Peter George Spackman, before retirement, enjoyed a variety of diverse occupations concluding in 27 years as a civil servant. Since retirement, the author has obtained a BA (Hons) from the University of Leicester, following a lifelong interest in History and Archaeology and published an enlightening book *An A-Z of 1001 Field-Names and Their Interpretation*. His hobbies are as varied as his life, actively engaging in archaeological investigations, history, intermingled with an appetite for a good game of poker and a passion for home-cooked food.

I dedicate this book to the victims of bullying, in whatever form, with the expectations of inducing the unfortunate fact that they are not alone and that someone somewhere is thinking of you.

Peter George Spackman

THE ADVENTURES
OF JONATHAN

TALES OF LIFE,
LOVE AND MORALITY

Peter G. Spackman 2019

AUSTIN MACAULEY PUBLISHERS™

LONDON • CAMBRIDGE • NEW YORK • SHARJAH

A CIP catalogue record for this title is available from the British Library.

ISBN 9781528908375 (Paperback)
ISBN 9781528908382 (Hardback)
ISBN 9781528908399 (E-Book)

www.austinmacauley.com

First Published (2019)
Austin Macauley Publishers Ltd
25 Canada Square
Canary Wharf
London
E14 5LQ

Unfortunately, without 'the bullies' and the parent of Jonathan, who subjected 'life lessons' upon an innocent child, for whatever reason, Jonathan would not have experienced 'refuge'. So, actually, in a roundabout way, without me condoning bullying, thank you for the people who bullied Jonathan.

A big thank you to Jonathan for allowing me to record and transcribe a few of his many lives, with the hope that he survives long enough to recall many more lives, loves and morals.

Thank you for the dedication and understanding of the illustrator Jacqueline Simester www.Illustrere.co.uk, her interpretation of my initial thoughts, her design techniques bringing the stories to life and adding a visual concept to the script.

Thank you to Stephen Wass, who, amongst many other talents, plays the squeezebox in a 'Morris Dancing Troup' for the task of composing the score to 'The Song of the Sweeps'.

Most of all, a huge thank you to my dear wife, Carol Ann, for the many hours that she supported and encouraged me whilst I put the tales of Jonathan on paper. Carol Ann is an angel amongst mortals, for whom I have had the honour and privilege to share five decades 'of this life' with a thought 'have we met before' in another time, another place.

Table of Contents

List of Illustrations

Poetry and Proses

Lyrics

Music Scope

Introduction

These are tales told by Jonathan, a person who was the victim of prolonged bullying, but Jonathan is not alone as the perpetrators (who I believe must carry a sort of bullying disease) are more numerous than people realise. A disease carried by unthoughtful people, whose only pleasure is to make someone sad as a result of being the subject of unkindness and both mental and physical cruelty. There are thousands of others, of all ages, out there in the wide, wide world who are constantly under the stress caused by bullying. It appears to be a perplexing situation in so much that the victim has little choice; do they complain to someone in authority and in so doing, may make matters worse for themselves, or do they retaliate in a way but in so doing, this places them at a far greater risk of harm. Sometimes, there are no easy options; sometimes, the only option is to grin and bear it; which, unfortunately, should not be an option at all. Jonathan does take the latter path but also develops some long-term strategies which could help him achieve an amicable outcome. In the recollections of Jonathan, you, the reader, will see how the strategy unfolds often in mysterious ways; it is not a magic in practice but magical in transition. You need to understand that Jonathan is not only bullied outside of the home but lives with a certain amount of fear, inside of the home. With the instances he recalls of physical abuse from an early age, little things like very hot water poured from a jug during hair washing with the instructions of 'stop the whinging', and the constant hard tapping of the top of his head when a parent was making a point. He remembers having some unsightly blister-like things on the knees for which the doctor had prescribed hot poultices to be applied each evening. This, he said was literally torture as the poultices were so hot that one parent had to use tongs to lift them from boiling water onto Jonathan's knees whilst the other parent looked on with tears in the eyes. It came to light years later that the reason for these torturous activities was to make Jonathan strong and brave, 'yeh' right. These activities only developed quite inward persona which in turn, Jonathan believed, signalled an open invitation to be bullied outside as well as inside of the home.

Say no to bullying.

Prologue

These are tales of life, its ups and downs, its expectations and the realities, the hidden mysteries of mind and beyond. This is the truth that develops, stems from the microcosm of eternal ether for which access is denied by the majority of souls but the few that have ventured into what I call *Quercusroburism:* the act of 'open mind' know this to be true; this is the reality of things, and reality is truth, is it not?

There are things that are truly unexplained, things which appear magical, and the secret is to offer no attempt of explanation but just to accept and learn that for every action, there is a reaction; sometimes, it is the unexpected outcome that inspires the recipient to greater things and develop a form of 'sixth sense'.

Let us begin; whether Jonathan is real or not, I leave entirely up to the reader to make up their own mind as I do not wish to influence anyone in any way, but merely tell the story as it happened.

Jonathan had just moved into a new house which, unlike the two-bedroomed dwelling he had shared with five adults and three children, was now a spacious three bedroomed and had the pleasure of a bathroom, all be it, downstairs. A small bedroom was all his with two sisters sharing another; overlooking a railway station as the semi-detached house was part of a new estate set upon a hill on the outskirts of town. A window gave a fascinating picture of the toing and froing of steam trains, some pulling multitudes of coal-filled wagons, which Jonathan used to count, and I remember him saying that the record number of wagons was 104. I think that Jonathan could count before being able to talk; that came at a price, as a small boy out of bed and staring through the window at trains was met with the displeasure of his father. That was not the worst thing to happen, and it was all too easy to accept punishment. I think if a person knows no alternative, that becomes the accepted norm; it becomes apparent that punishment is the result of something that someone somewhere believes to be wrong, but are not steam trains beautiful beasts, not to be missed and worthy of a smack or two.

It was night time that hid the fears; yes, the dark and unknown can be very worrisome; especially if there are things that are not explained. Jonathan recalled the first time he saw a ghost, the ghost of his great-grandmother when an apparition appeared ascending, swaying side to side a white-faced staring figure tapering into nothingness, not evil but most definitely frightening. The first year after that was bad; there were visions and happenings, Jonathan put his head into his hands and recalls nights of noises, shuffling sounds and realistic attacks by large black birds. Sleeping under the covers, afraid to even peek out until the blessing of day light; those early years were nothing more than mental torture with no escape, nights seemed a never-ending torment. Almost as if the house and particularly that room had been placed on some ancient burial ground where bodies were laid on pyres, open air and subjected to repeated visits of carrion crows ripping the flesh from the departed; memories all relived in the very fabric of the earth and transmitted, somehow, through the bricks and mortar to the souls who dwell inside.

School would be an escape from 'the house' or so Jonathan thought, but it did not take many weeks for the bullies to latch on, like hungry leaches, and soon he was a victim of not only name-calling but physical abuse. It is, unfortunately, a reality that children try to dominate, rule and influence others who tend not to possess those traits. Just a fact of life, I guess but not an acceptable one, and all that we can do is endure with a resolute mind and more than a little hope. It is apparent that if you know of nothing else, you accept your life as a normality and make of it as best as you can. It is funny that during the, supposedly, age of innocence that there are many who were found to be lacking in the art of compassion and love, and many who are found lacking as recipients of the same.

Jonathan tells me that one of the ways to escape was to leave the body, take the mind elsewhere, and how he would be 'off fishing' during school assembly and walking through tranquil woodland listening to the birds singing; smelling the fragrant blossoms of chestnut, elderberry and thorn. This, according to Jonathan, could, with a little practice, be done at will and offered a welcome respite from the real world, and he was convinced that this was not an actual dream nor make-believe but actual happenings that took place in different places, even in different times.

It was soon realised that this practice of escape was often greeted with more ridicule and was best done away from prying eyes, for it was more than a little disconcerting to see someone apparently come out of some sort of trance and suddenly returned from a form of sleep. This is why when Jonathan found a hidden refuge, a place which acted almost as a sanctuary, he took advantage. In a wooded knoll thick with bramble, Jonathan, on one of his walks, had come across an abandoned shopping trolley, deep, safe and a refuge from the ugly world; this was to be the place from which the stories would begin, this was the place from which Jonathan would live life after life and develop mind, body and soul. Jonathan had found a well of journeys, happenings, adventures and knowledge from which to sip and blossom. The trolley was one of the deeper variety, snug fitting, safe, secure and a haven to which Jonathan became attached as if this was a magical place. The place that became a path to a different world, worlds of unimaginable lives and prospective hopes to which Jonathan, alone held the key. He explained that it did not take him long to realise that the body was merely material to house the brain, and the brain was operative and functioning at the behest of the soul, and it is the soul that travels outside of the body whether it be forward or backward to the present time.

These are not just tales but realities; these happened, and I am the lucky one, chosen by Jonathan, to write the words that tell the truths of 'Life, Love and Morality'.

Chapter 1
The Hollow Stacks

Players: Gheghedo, Suemo, Love, Quirsler, Reah, Bartib, Tapeloc, Darbeg, Greatbelonda, Grasylee, Tar.

The summer holidays are here, and there are thoughts of seaside trips, walking, exploring, cycling and fishing; Jonathan will have plenty to do during the seven week break. One thing that Jonathan and his friends enjoyed was fishing, and the three of them rode on their bicycles just a couple of miles along the bank of the local river. It was a quiet afternoon, just the birds singing and a few moo's from nearby cows, and when parking the three bikes behind a hedge, the trout could be seen rising catching flies and bugs from the surface. This was Jonathan's away time, a time to relax and a time to savour the peace of the countryside. With a creel around his shoulder, a folding landing net clipped on his belt and a beautiful greenheart rod in his hand. Jonathan accompanied his two friends to the river bank in anticipation of a good day. Indeed, after a couple of hours more than a dozen trout were in the creel, so that was two each and six for the local fishmonger who payed ten shillings a pound for fresh fish, and this money was shared between the three anglers. Back home, it was Friday night, and that meant it was the day of the red-hot poultices, not a thing that Jonathan looked forward to, but there was no other option but to endure certain pain. Just before bedtime, into the living room comes father with a pan in which the poultices had been bubbling away. The pan was placed on the floor whilst Jonathan obeys the commands and stretches out his legs onto a small pouffe; father, using wooden tongs because the poultices were far too hot to handle with bare hands, but apparently not too hot for the knees of Jonathon. The poultices were lifted from the pan and placed directly on the exposed knees; that hurt, that was pure pain which brought tears to the eyes of Jonathan but not a sound is uttered by Jonathan who had learnt not to cry out as this would only aggravate the situation. The large blisters were cured by the poultices, but it did take about five treatments. 'Treatments' was not the phrase Jonathan used to describe this 'cruelty' which would not have been acceptable in modern day society. Saturday was chore day, and Jonathan had to chop up logs to supply tinder for the four fires inside the house; this was actually fun but did incur occasional small cuts. Chores done Jonathan readies for a bike ride and will first cycle over to one of his friend's house and luckily finds him in; they decide to go to the large green by the river where there are always lots of picnickers. The pair are going there to recover as many empty lemonade bottles that they could find because there is a bounty on bottle returns from a half to one penny. The bottles soon mount up and are hidden in undergrowth to be collected at the end of the day when the total was near one hundred and fifty. One of Jonathan's friends had a two-wheeled bogey, like a box on wheels, which could be attached to the back of the bicycle. When the price of fish and chips was around twenty-four pence, one pound eight shillings collected from the bottles was the equivalent to 336 pennies; that was a lot of fish and chips, great fun. The pair sit in the market place eating their hard earnt meal when they are approached by three of the regular bullies, and there is no obvious escape. Gone are the fish and chips, stolen by the bullies, but that is not the end of this confrontation, and there is little that the two bottle collectors could do as the three assailants made off with a delicious meal but also took the bicycles. This was bad news as there would be repercussions when Jonathan returned home; this was not a secret that he could keep from his parents, notably the father. In fear of a beating for losing his bike, Jonathan sought the sanctuary of his hideaway and the shopping trolley, wondering just what he had done to deserve such ill will and malice as he drifts off into escapism and an apparent relief from upset and pain.

Jonathan opens his eyes and is now in a dark place; it feels a little claustrophobic, and there is a strong aroma of burning, damp soot and coal. There in one of the walls that could be seen, high up; one small window which brightens as the sun rises burning through morning mist and smog. Looking around this bare-bricked room, he could see that it is probably a cellar, and there are other two occupants covered with black sacks and only strands of unkempt hair identifying their presence. Jonathan is now Gheghedo, a young boy aged about nine years. The parents of Gheghedo had died in a tragic accident just over four years ago, and he had been brought up and looked after by an Aunt called Love and her husband named Darbeg, who had one child of their own; a hard working eight-year-old girl named Suemo. They were a very poor family with very limited income, and because of this, they had to sell the two children in their care, Suemo and Gheghedo, for three guineas to a local master sweep. Gheghedo has worked for about eighteen months as a boy sweep, so is fairly experienced but thin and unkempt. The other two children in the cellar are also young sweeps, although, they were a little older. Reah a ten year-old-girl and Tapeloc, her brother, who at eleven was the oldest; both had been purchased from the workhouse. There is no mention of Gheghedo's step-sister Suemo or what actually happened to her after she was sold to the Master Sweep; a scowling man, barely thirty years of age, known as Quirsler. I suppose, as she was very proficient in house-keeping and chores, Suemo may well have been resold as some sort of domestic servant; Gheghedo often thinks of her. Suemo is really the nearest thing to a family member he could ever remember.

This cellar is cold, damp and inhospitable, but now, this is 'home' and somewhere that, or so the other occupants state, 'will be home until they reach the age of eighteen'. Apparently, by that age, the young sweeps would be far too big to fit inside a chimney (apart from one of the massive medieval fireplaces) and, indeed, considered lucky to have reached that age at all. All three have now awoken and are looking like three urchins prepared for the day ahead. There is no food yet, until Quirsler arrives and unlocks the cellar door, as this was to prevent any escape. I suppose, it is understandable as three young sweeps are bought and payed for. The sun could just be seen through the window as another day began, and it was not long before the rattling of keys was heard, and the thought of food occupied the mind. The door creaked and jerked as it struggled to open, and the dark silhouetted figure of the Master Sweep stands tall in the doorway. Presented to the three was a soot-stained wicker basket which acted as a nest for a loaf of bread, an offering that had seen better days, but this was all they received, each day, every day. There was also a large ceramic pitcher filled to the brim with water but just one wooden cup, eagerly shared. Gheghedo thought it best to devour the morsel whilst the cellar was still in partial darkness as the sight of the mold which grew on, through and under the fairly hard bread would have been a turn off (I suppose, the green bits could be classed as one of the five a day vegetables, the only one). This meal was sometimes the only meal of the day, and any extra food was begged from the kitchen of the houses to which the young sweeps were sent; this is called living hand to mouth. No need to get dressed ready for the day because the three young sweeps only have one set of clothes which are worn night and day, and lucky, if they own a pair of shoes. I suppose, the lack of food keeps them thin enough to climb inside the narrow chimneys, so they were actually, intentionally, deprived of much-needed sustenance. The three were taken by horse and cart to a large country house which would be the first job of the day; each have a hard-bristled hand brush, a metal scraper, a leather hat and of course, the obligatory black sacks (the latter actually doubled as their blankets); these were the tools of the trade. No goggles, no knee pads, no breathing apparatus, but this house does have a fountain, on a small island in the centre of a lake, set amongst a 'garden of diversion'. That was certainly something to look forward to (if there was time) as washing was at the most something that took place four times a year, if you were lucky. Looking upwards, Gheghedo could see many chimneys; just how many, he did not know as he could not count, but as many as his fingers, and nor could either of the two companions as none of the three had ever been to school. The chimneys looked to be all of different designs, all about the same height, but the patterns changed from stack to stack.

Quirsler, the Master Sweep, did not waste time in allocating the first three chimneys; he himself does nothing, but direct the children and make sure there is no slacking, as time is money. This house, or should we call it a mansion, would take at least three days to complete, and the young sweeps would have to sleep in one of the hay barns; this would be no hardship as it would be a lot cleaner than their cellar back in the city.

Three sweeps asleep in the cellar.

Tapeloc was taken to one of the main rooms which actually had a really old fireplace almost four yards across and the home to a very large fire grate. The fireplace was still emitting a little warmth which meant that the chimney would be equally warm if not hotter; this was a hard one to start with, and there is no arguing with Quirsler just grin and bear it. Tapeloc is set to clearing the grate so as to stop any smoke from the embers choking his lungs on the way up the hollow stack. Next to this large room was another in which there could be seen a smaller fireplace which, thank goodness, had not been used for a couple of days but had a narrow shaft. In this small gap went Gheghedo, brush and scraper in hand and was pushed by Quirsler who then partially blocked the opening to stop any soot escaping into the room. It should not take longer than twenty minutes until Gheghedo reaches the top, and this has to be done very quickly as the fresh air would be waiting when Gheghedo sees the light of the sky.

On the way up, it was a matter of scraping off the embedded soot and tar formed by burning wood and coal from all four sides. There were some stubborn lumps of coal tar, and it was obvious to Gheghedo that the chimneys were well overdue for the attention of a sweep. What was missed on the way up would be tackled on the way down which involved running fingers along the side walls of the stack; it was pitch black inside, and not long before the eyes felt the annoyance of fine powdered soot. The knack was to close the eyes as soon as they ascended upwards, breath as little as possible and work as fast as you could. Gheghedo could feel fresh air as he neared to the top; so the art was to gulp in as much as possible because going down, the scraper and hard brush would be working feverishly; powered by arms working like the blades of a windmill on a stormy night. The bottom was reached, and there the sweep would call out 'ahoy, ahoy'; this was a signal for Quirsler to remove the sack from the front of the grate.

This was an odd call but the rumour was that Quirsler had a longing to be a ship's captain and preferred to be addressed as 'captain', and the sweep to shout ahoy to alert him that the sweep was nearing the lower part of the shaft.

Majestic hollow stacks.

That was also a signal for Reah to clear the soot and debris using a small shovel and fill the sack with all the soot and anything else that comes down and with a quick brush of the grate that was one finished; the bad thing was, it took twice as long as it should. Obviously, Quirsler was either mistaken or was he hoodwinked by the owner as to the date of the last sweeping of these chimneys. To add to the already increased time was the fact that Gheghedo had to clear the lungs and the immersing of the head into a nearby trough of spring water in an effort to clear the eyes was essential and then off to the next chimney. Passing back through the large room, the scraping by Tapeloc could be heard deep into the heart of the shaft, or should we say shafts; this large fireplace actually had three shafts emanating branch-like from the main grate, and two distinct piles of soot could be seen already waiting to be cleared, meaning that he was in the last shaft of three. Reah, after taking one sack outside, was soon back and ready with two more sacks to fill with soot and grime from the large chimney from which could be seen dangling, two black feet belonging to Tapeloc, soon to be followed by a coughing and sputtering apparition of a being; so covered in soot, you could not tell which way around he was. Reah brushed down the head of her brother and removed as much of the soot as she could before he could walk without leaving an obvious trail behind on the wooden floor. One thing that Reah mentioned to Gheghedo, in passing, is that she had seen one of the kitchen maids and arranged some morsels that had been left over from the previous night's meal but made doubly sure that Quirsler knew nothing of the arrangement or else, the three sweeps would see nothing of the food. The maid would bring whatever she could to the barn just before nightfall; now that was something worth its weight in gold. Jonathan recollects that the very thought of a wash and a meal, on the same day, was a momentous occasion and something that the three would dream of for a long, long, long time.

Tapeloc had a slight grin with thoughts of proper food as he made his way to the next room, and luckily, this fire was cold, which was a blessing as there were a couple of burn marks visible on the arms along with a noticeable graze on the forehead now embedded with black grime. The side rooms are a more modern addition to the central, large Tudor rooms, and the chimneys were more vertical, culminating in tall stacks and hopefully, less soot. This room had a fire place at each end; maybe, it was at one time two smaller rooms; there was no time to waste as Quirsler entered the room and prompted both Tapeloc and Gheghedo to scamper up a chimney each. The first couple of yards were used as a respite when the young sweeps took an out of sight rest from constant toil, and as long as the scrapers could be heard, Quirsler was happy; which in itself was a rare occurrence indeed. The soot on the inside of these two chimneys was particularly loose, so there was a more-than-average chance of slipping back down, and shoes were more of a hindrance and were quickly kicked off to effect a better grip with their bare toes. The shoes were immediately collected by Reah before they were buried beneath the ever-increasing avalanche of fine, rather acrid, jet-black soot. The thought of some food kept them going, and after another four chimneys each, the end of the day was approaching, and reluctantly, Quirsler called an end to the day. The Master Sweep stressed discontent as only a quarter of the total number of chimneys had been cleaned, and it was looking like this house would take four days to complete, and time costs money. Leaving the three sweeps secured in one of the barns at the large house, Quirsler headed back to the city, stipulating that the start would be an early one, and that they would need extra help to get back on track. Sat amongst the hay, Gheghedo, Reah and Tapeloc knew exactly who the 'help' would be, and that was a rather obnoxious boy called Tar. They had met Tar on only one other occasion, and that meeting had literally left scars not only on the body but also imprinted on the mind. But, that was tomorrow, and these three intrepid sweeps thought only of the day and in unison headed for the nearby lake. The sun was down but still light enough to see where they were going and soon all that could be seen was three neat piles of clothes and ripples spreading across the lake. In the centre of the lake was a fountain to which Reah swam, leaving the other two non-swimmers splashing about in the shallows. Reah waved as an indication of achievement by reaching the fountain and discovering a small rowing boat complete with a pair of oars jumped in and rowed back to the lake's edge. It did not take long to get rid of most of the soot, but the three could still be seen with ingrained soot on their feet, lower arms and heads; this took more than one wash to remove, if at all. They soon dried in the evening breeze and dressed again, but with encrusted soot and grime upon their clothes, in no time at all, the three looked like they had never been in the lake, but you can't miss an opportunity for a good wash.

Back at the barn the three sorted out their beds using the soft fresh hay; the scene looked as if three large birds had constructed three giant nests. There could be heard a creak as the barn door slowly opened, and a head poked around the corner and whispered, "It is Grasylee from the kitchen Reah. Reah are you there?" The kitchen maid had arrived and in her hand was a picnic basket, and she handed it over to Reah who in turn thanked her profusely. Grasylee departed and left the door of the barn open, so there was a little light permeating the inside of the barn. Reah placed the picnic basket in the centre of the barn on the flagstones; over walked Gheghedo and Tapeloc who, in unison, lifted the lid of the wicker basket to reveal a patterned cloth under which it could be seen that the basket was filled to the brim with all sort of food. This was heaven; this was goodness at its best, and when Tapeloc pulled out a large lamb bone, there was, in harmony, a cry of 'wow' because there was large amounts of meat still on the bone, all cooked to perfection.

Up until this day, even the actual smell of something cooking was a rarity, never mind holding such a delicacy.

Tapeloc took a huge bite and lay back upon a pile of hay and chewed and chewed until his taste buds were bursting in delight, and there was drooling taking place as pearls of saliva slowly descended from both corners of his mouth. There was fruit, bread, cake and a jug of fresh milk; the latter quickly disappeared down the sooty throats of these undernourished excuses for humanity. The contents of the 'basket of delights' gradually diminished, but there was enough for another day; the only trouble was to keep it well hidden from Quirsler and the pending appearance of Tar. On this extremely rare occasion, there was a mutual feeling of joy, fulfilment and a small glimpse of 'the meaning of life'. Gheghedo started to hum a tune which caused Reah to grab a pebble and tap out a rhythm on a piece of wood, and Tapeloc put down his well-chewed lamb bone, raising his weary body and performed a jig, and Gheghedo sang a song.

The lake and fountain in full flow.

For the young sweeps, this evening was an exhibition of pure happiness; if anyone had spotted them in those few minutes of escapism, it would have definitely given a false impression of their harsh and cruel existence. Settled for the night, Gheghedo turned his weary head, and there to be seen in the flickering candlelight were the smiles of children who had been robbed of their childhood, stolen by a society which had not developed the meaning of care for the underprivileged. Covering themselves with more hay, Gheghedo, Reah and Tapeloc smiled at each other, nothing was said; the looks upon their faces were enough to relate to this rare moment of pleasure, and as far as they were concerned, an indulgence that may never pass their way again. The nests were dry, warm and a much-needed luxury but to them an extravagance; they (the innocent sweeps) all slept well that night from the exuberant, rare pleasures of enjoyment.

(Authors note) So simple, to modern day people, were these 'sweep's luxuries' in so much, it is hard to imagine the hardships of years ago, and everyday items today are taken for granted. This gives an insight into the hearts and minds of the millions that have not even a bale of hay to lay on, a gulp of fresh milk to cure a thirst or even just an apple to enjoy. What it is like is hard to imagine unless you experience the same hardships, the same fears; from this awareness emanates the birth of charity, humility and kindness, and there should be no time for war, sadness and grief.

The morning was greeted by the sound of the dawn chorus, of birdsong, a loveliness in itself; never had the young sweeps heard such a mystical noise in all of their numbered years. A thirst-quenching drink from the hand pump by the trough gave the sweeps a refreshing start and a piece of bread each before hiding the basket amongst the hay, and at least, there was a meal to look forward to. Quirsler arrived shortly afterwards with Tar on his side. Tar was approaching the age of eighteen so was virtually a qualified sweep who would one day soon have his own team of poor wretches to send to work. It was noted by Gheghedo that Tar appeared to be a little too wide at the shoulders to climb inside the shafts of the vast majority of the chimneys so it was strange that Quirsler had brought him along to help.

The Song of the Sweeps (AKA Tapeloc's Song)

(1)
O Sweep O Sweep O Sweep O
I brush and scrape each brick and crack
O Sweep O Sweep O Sweep O
Our place is in your chimney stack

(2)
No shoes or socks, no buttons on my shirt
With a hey ho nonny nonny no no no
Put your knees in the air and dance with me
With a hey ho nonny nonny no

(03)
O Sweep O Sweep O Sweep O
I climb and grope towards the light
O Sweep O Sweep O Sweep O
As doth a moth in dark of night

(04)
No money or a purse and living with a curse
With a hey ho nonny nonny no no no
Put your knees in the air and dance with me

(06)
No friends or kin and grimy soot for a skin
With a hey ho nonny nonny no no no
Put your knees in the air and dance with me
With a hey ho nonny nonny no

(07)
O Sweep O Sweep O Sweep O
I long to be a child of play
O Sweep O Sweep O Sweep O
Another life, another day

(08)
No hope or fresh air just heaps of despair
With a hey ho nonny nonny no no no
Put your knees in the air and dance with me
With a hey ho nonny nonny no

(09)
O Sweep O Sweep O Sweep O
I worry not of money food or rest
O Sweep O Sweep O Sweep O

With a hey ho nonny nonny
no

(05)

O Sweep O Sweep O Sweep
O
I breathe but dust with lungs
afire
O Sweep O Sweep O Sweep
O
My life is not what I desire

I clean, I scrape and do my
best

(10)

No shoes or socks no buttons
on my shit
With a hey ho nonny nonny
no no no
Put your knees in the air and
dance with me
With a hey ho nonny nonny
no

The Song of the Sweeps

The three sweeps dancing in the barn.

The fireplaces today were on the second floor comprising of two large and many narrow, and it was the large that they tackled first. Unfortunately, one of them had been is use the night before and to say that the grate and chimney were warm would have been an understatement; this one was given to Gheghedo and helper would-be Tar. Gheghedo set to clearing the embers, some still glowing from the grate and wanted to leave it an hour for the heat to abate, but Tar would have none of it, and there was no arguing if you are a young sweep. Jonathan relates with a combined look of disgust and ear, showed a little difficulty in relaying this event. Gheghedo commenced with his scraper in one hand and brush in the other and had wrapped a pieces of torn sack around his hands but already the heat was near unbearable and stated that it was too hot to climb. As the feet of Gheghedo were still showing, Tar was having none of this and had been instructed by the Master Sweep Quirsler to speed thing up, and out of his pocket, Tar produced one of the 'tools of the trade'. This tool was to 'encourage' a sweep in a difficult situation; the tool was a small stick in which inserted into one end were two or three sharp pins that would be used to prod the soles of the feet of the unlucky sweep, hence giving an incentive to climb further into the chimney. There was only one way to go, and one very quick clean of this chimney; so now it became very clear to everyone why the presence of Tar was required. Gheghedo was up and down in quick fashion sweating profusely and ran/limped straight to the trough into which he placed his feet which looked a little worse for wear. Pinpricking was not an uncommon practice in the world of chimney sweeping, and not the first time that one of them had experienced such an enticement. It was bad enough having the soles of your feet stabbed by sharp pins but to hear the chortling offerings coming from the mouth of Tar was not at all cherishing to the heart. It was not until later in the morning that Gheghedo met up with the others, and it was clear that Reah had experienced the same treatment when struggling into one of the narrow shafts just a few rooms away and the resulting blood could be seen on the cloth rags Reah had wrapped around her tender feet. The only good thing was that progress had caught up to the deadline, but at what cost? Is there a price on pain? Is there a price on cruelty? Such is the life, as a sweep. Next was an all-out effort as all three young sweeps were escorted to, perhaps the largest fireplace, and the great structure dominating the kitchen. This had to be done fairly quickly as it would be needed to cook the evening meal, and it soon became apparent that this chimney had had more than one resent fall of soot and was probably the reason why the sweeps had been brought to this country mansion in the first place. This chimney was split into two shafts into which Tapeloc and Gheghedo ventured; the inside was still warm but not unbearable, and it took a while to clear the soot from the flattish areas that could be found on either side of the fireplace, about eighteen inches inside the chimney, just before the shafts split and rose near vertically into the darkness. It was futile to carry a candle as the updraft and dust would extinguish the flame in a matter of seconds as well as needing three pairs of arms. In the left shaft, Tapeloc cleared fallen soot to reveal the remains of a cat, mummified and well-preserved; the owner was called to the scene, in case the house had lost a cat in the past. The owner Lady Greatbelonda knew of the cat and explained that it was placed there intentionally after it had died many years ago, for the purpose of warding off evil spirits. There, alongside the cat, was a small pair of leather shoes which Lady G's parents had put there when she had grown out of them at the age of five; now, that must have been at least seventy years ago. The shoes too were used as a device to protect the house from witches who were believed to enter properties through openings such as chimneys. These two items, at the bequest of the owner, were to be replaced on the ledge after the two shafts were cleaned. Tapeloc soon realised that the reason that the soot accumulated in the first place was because of the rough stonework inside the shaft; most of the stone blocks were rough, and some protruded a few inches creating small areas where the soot could accumulate; this was a really old chimney with no bricks at all. The owner left the kitchen with both Tar and Quirsler in tow, probably to show them where the next rooms were. Gheghedo removed the soot from the shelf of the right-hand shaft expecting another object placed there to protect the household from ogres, witches and evil spirits, but only soot was to be found. It was not until Gheghedo was slightly higher that he felt a small recess which was clogged with soot and removed the hardened mass with his scraper, only to hear a metallic sound. He thought little of it because chimneys have been known to contain metal braces to stabilise loose stonework. He put his fingers into the crevice only to feel a small metal tin, only about three or four inches square which he placed in his pocket. Up they went scraping and brushing, and it was evident that both shafts had caught fire in the past as the soot in places had turned very hard, and the scrapers worked overtime to scrape away lumps of stubborn sooty encrustations. One of the practices that the owners of coal-fired fireplaces was to deliberately set fire on soot low down in the shaft, and let the resulting flames travel up the chimney, therefore, eliminating loose, dusty soot and replacing it with a hard tar-like crusty surface; this could have happened in this chimney but the amount of soot was probably a little too much. Reah was kept busy emptying the fireplace of avalanches of soot and hard crusty lumps and filled over nine bags with the stuff. Both these shafts, because of the hard lumps, had been the cause of scuffed knuckles, bruised elbows and knees, but that was all in a day's work. A quick break allowed for the three to compare injuries, almost with pride, as each showed their battle scars. Copious amounts of spring water was drank, half of which was spontaneously coughed up, not at all pleasant, but it was the bodies way of clearing the undesirable, harmful substances from their precious, essential airways. The afternoon of the second day saw the three young sweeps move to the upstairs rooms which have much narrower shafts but half the vertical distance to travel. Two of the chimneys measured little more than 10 inches square, and this warranted a change in the technical approach by entering hands first, above the head; in one hand, a brush and in the other, a scraper. The only problem was that everything came down on to the head so the best thing to do was to wear one of the soot sacks on the head with the overhang covering the eyes. Gheghedo was the lucky one as his shaft was a little wider but not much and prepared accordingly just like Reah and Tapeloc who looked a little apprehensive. Reah went first, arms up and scraping from the start, but it was not too long before she ran into trouble; she was stuck. Tapeloc and Gheghedo ran to her aid and managed to pull her free; gasping for air, Reah with head back breathed deeply. At that moment, Tar entered the room to investigate the commotion, saw what was happening and ordered Tapeloc to go up the very chimney from which Reah was rescued. In those days, no one argued with those above, and Tapeloc duly obliged with the obligatory sack upon his head, equipment in each hand. In he went and managed OK, until his hips proved a little too wide and shouts of anguish could be heard. It appeared that Tapeloc was wedged in the same position as Reah was a few moments ago. Through the doorway walked Tar who eyed up the situation, and his solution was a little frightening, to say the least. A fire was lit, by Tar, beneath the feet of Tapeloc; there was a crackling as the small wooden tinder caught hold and flames flickered and danced around the feet of Tapeloc, accompanied by ear-shattering yells of pain. The pair of small feet danced desperately for a few moments as if they were dancing to the tune of the night previous, before disappearing upwards into the shaft. A grin appeared on the face of Tar who cynically uttered the words that Jonathan would never forget as long as he lived, and they were, "That worked, didn't it?" Tar turned and looked at Gheghedo who immediately and with some speed entered the shaft which he had descended from to help the poor wretched Tapeloc. There was no sound from the narrow shaft which worried Gheghedo somewhat as he scraped feverishly away, brushing like a mad person to get the job done before a fire was lit beneath himself. It was not long before he could see daylight at the top of the tall chimney and after a few deep breaths, descended with head bowed and soot falling all over. There was a sound from the third chimney, but nothing could be heard from the room where Tapeloc was working; as Gheghedo called out, Reah answered and confirmed that she was alright and almost finished. Together they cleared the soot from the grates of the two chimneys that they had cleaned into a sack and together carried it out into the courtyard of the house. Just in time, to see both Quirsler and Tar loading sacks onto the cart, and Tar cracked his whip setting the two horses on their way, and the wagon, at top speed, soon disappeared up the gravelled drive. Quirsler turned to see Gheghedo and Reah and immediately directed them back into the manor house and to the next two stacks. Reah did inquire as to the whereabouts of her brother, Tapeloc and was told that he had been taken to another more urgent job a few miles away and would not be back for a few days. Another few hours passed as the two remaining saddened soiled sweeps swiftly-stacked several sooty sacks signalling that this working day was drawing to an end. After a wash at the water pump, Gheghedo walked solemnly back to the barn with Reah, not uttering a word, but there was an air of actual fear and despondency descending as a fog-like shroud around them. Gheghedo recovered the hidden basket from the hay, and the two ate and drank what they could, keeping back some morsels for the absent and missed Tapeloc. Just before they were thinking of curling up in their nests of hay, there was a small tap, tap on the barn door, a recognisable sound to which Reah responded. It was the kitchen maid Grasylee with another hamper, and she had been very careful not to raise any suspicion and added that Quirsler, luckily, was sleeping in the servants quarters that evening. Reah explained that Tapeloc had left, and that this is most likely their last night at the manor house as there were only six more chimneys to sweep. Before she left, Grasylee requested that the empty baskets were ready to be returned early in the morning, and that she would come to the barn before first light. There were feelings of concern for Tapeloc because he would normally not have left without a departing word; Gheghedo added some words of comfort to Reah before lying down amongst the hay. The lump in his pocket, as he lay down, brought back thoughts of the small box, and Gheghedo took it out of his pocket. It was heavier than he first remembered, and the top of the box was proving difficult to remove, but that would wait until tomorrow when the light was better. Gheghedo placed the box next to his chest, pulled the hay over himself and thought of Tapeloc, his friend, his missing friend, one of only two friends he knew.

The morning arrives only too soon, and after gorging themselves with food, the two sweeps were ready for whatever the day would bring. Thoughts of the small tin box took his mind off other things as Gheghedo lit a candle near the barn door, away from any hay and attempted to open the box, to no avail. An old rusty nail came to the rescue as he used it to force off the top, and this time with success; ping it went and flew across the slabs with a clatter quickly followed by the contents. On the ground was a small bundle which Gheghedo picked up, inquisitively; the little bundle was quite heavy for its size, and on unwrapping, there, in the candlelight, glinting and shining were strange coins, gold coins, twenty or more. Reah, who was preparing the baskets, looked over and walked across the barn to look; all they could do was look at each other, then at the coins and back to each other. Gheghedo soon decided that they should not give them to either Tar, if they even see him again, or even Quirsler and that they should be given to Lady Greatbelonda. That would be almost impossible as a simple lowly sweep could not approach such a Lady, but Reah suggested that she give the box and coins to Grasylee when she came for the hampers, who could then pass them on to the Lady Greatbelonda. It was not long before the candlelight flickered out, as Gheghedo prepared the sacks for the day ahead, and Reah waited by the barn door; with the hampers Grasylee appeared, but Quirsler was not far behind so Reah, very quickly, told the story of the box and coins placed them into one of the hampers, and Grasylee swiftly disappeared around the opposite corner of the barn so as not to be seen by Quirsler.

On approaching the barn door, Quirsler was shouting in a rather angry voice and wanted to know why Reah and Gheghedo were not at the main house working. The two young sweeps apologised and ran out carrying their tools and arms full of sacks, actually sprinting to the house. Today, instead of two chimneys each between three of them, it was three chimney apiece because Tapeloc was not with them. Quirsler wanted them finished as quickly as possible before returning to the city and thoughts of the damp, dark and uninviting cellar encroached on the mind and no resting until the tasks are complete. So, as fast as they could, Reah and Gheghedo tackled those last few hollow stacks with no thoughts other than to get the job done before the evil Tar returned, and the deadly needle prod saw the light of the day. These last few chimneys were of the narrow type, and the resulting grazed arms, knees and heads made the two sweeps appear like something from a distant battlefield and a war fought in a coal mine; they were black and bloodied; they were heroes. With one each to go, Quirsler was still trying to speed up the process and even filled the sacks so that Reah and Gheghedo could climb the last two narrow stacks. These last two chimneys were completed in record time, and as Gheghedo descended and squeezed out onto the fire place, he almost collapsed, and Quirsler yelled at him to get on with it, as they all had to leave as soon as he was paid. As Reah entered the room in which

Gheghedo and Quirsler were filling the last sack; the gardener preceded by the Lady Greatbelonda entered, and her presence was felt by all. A formidable women, a women of stature, poise and grace, with eyes that penetrated deep into the very soul of the recipient. She asked for Gheghedo by name. Quirsler stood between the Lady of the house and the young sweep and stated that whatever the boy had done, punishment would be dealt swift and harsh. Lady Greatbelonda looked Quirsler straight in the eye and raised her head, as if talking to his tall hat and told him to be silent and speak only at her request. "Come," she commanded, "come, Gheghedo, to the kitchen and the girl also," with such authority that obedience was assured. Leaving Quirsler to twiddle his agitated thumbs and pace nervously upon the oak flooring; this was beyond his control, and it showed on his worried brow.

The four of them left the room, one behind the other, with Lady Greatbelonda to the fore and on reaching the main kitchen, ushered the two sweeps to a table on which sat two baskets (the very same that Reah, Tapeloc and Gheghedo had enjoyed these past couple of nights).

At this point, Jonathan tells me that he thought there was trouble ahead, and that they would most definitely be punished for eating the contents of the hampers, and that the kitchen maid Grasylee would be thrown out.

Lady Greatbelonda looked Gheghedo in the eyes and commanded him to sit on the table and then uttered the same command to Reah. The next command was to the gardener, whose apt name was Flowerdale, to speak of the night previous when he saw something moving near the small copse next to the lake. Flowerdale, in his deep rustic voice, told of two figures in dark clothes digging a hole, and the shorter of the two placing something that was tipped from the back of a cart, what looked like, a black sack and proceeded to fill in the hole. The faces of the two figures were not seen by Flowerdale as it was too dark, and they moved hurriedly away; as the estate was often visited by a poacher or two, Flowerdale thought it was best investigated in the light of day. This he did and found a patch of freshly disturbed turf and was intrigued to find out what the poachers had been up to, and on removing a piece of turf, he removed about 30cms of soil to reveal the most harrowing sight; the body of a young boy, as black as soot. Reah yelps as her darkest thoughts turned to an unwelcoming truth, a million sorrows flashed across her face, a thousand tears flowed on her cheeks, a hundred groans filled the air; ten times she spoke my brother, my brother and a single arm that of a speechless Gheghedo held her tight. It appeared that Tapeloc had escaped the fires that burnt his feet but met a gruesome fate when trapped in the narrow hollow shaft. Lady Greatbelonda had already made arrangements for Tapeloc and showed compassion towards both the sweeps and consoled them this sad day. Provisions were made for both the sweeps to stay the night, and hot water was fetched to wash away, not only the soot but the blood from grazed and battered skin. Although Reah and Gheghedo were in more comfortable surroundings, little sleep they had that dark and dismal night. They talked and wept and talked some more, only too well they realised what wretched lives they lead and wondered now, not just of what the next day would bring but, indeed, what life they would have, next week, next month, next year.

The morning sun rose with the rays streaming through glass windows; the two sweeps stirred as Lady Greatbelonda entered the room inviting them to the kitchen for breakfast. They already knew that the baskets were there on the table, and with expectations of being told off for eating the food, they made their way to the kitchen. After bread, honey and some fruit, the Lady of the house beckoned towards the baskets. Lady Greatbelonda called for Grasylee; immediately, Gheghedo bowed his head in readiness for what was to come. Grasylee entered quietly and Lady G, instead of scolding the kitchen maid, referred to the baskets as the little gifts for the little sweeps, and with that, Gheghedo looked up. There was a sudden gasp from both Gheghedo and the kitchen maid as this was the first time they had seen each other because Reah had always accepted the baskets by the barn door. The cause of the gasp was a sudden realisation that Grasylee was actually Gheghedo's missing stepsister Suemo, and many hard years had passed since they were sold; what a truly amazing coincidence. Not that this reunion took from the sorrow, but it was great news, and sometimes when a person endures life rather than enjoys life, the heart is hardened to protect from emotions whether they are good or bad; these are the scares of life. Apparently, Lady Greatbelonda had a good heart and felt more than a modicum of responsibility for the young sweeps and brought forth the small box, the box that Gheghedo had found; but now cleaned and polished shining like new. Lady G thanked Gheghedo for his honesty before explaining what the coins were. Inside the tin there were placed 23 gold coins, and they were called Laurels from the reign of James 1 and were quite valuable. It was believed that the coins were hidden in the tin as protection from witches and acted as a payment to evil spirits; a sort of bribe to keep them away. This practice was confirmed by the designs etched into two sides of the tin; one design was called a '*Merel*' which looked like a flower with six petals and the other called a '*Pentacle*'; an offer was made by Lady Greatbelonda to Quirsler and by the look upon her face, an offer that could not be refused. The offer was one laurel each for the release of both sweeps and no payment for cleaning the chimneys because that money would be used to cover the cost of funeral of Tapeloc, and that was the only offer on the table. You could see that Quirsler was a little undecided but Lady G just had to mention that the local 'watchman' (now that person was the forerunner of a policeman) had been informed of the happenings witnessed by Flowerdale in the dark of night, and Quirsler had no option but to agree. There were also some rather unexpected offers on the table, and these indeed turned out to be as if it were ten birthdays all in a single day. The offers are all the work of Lady Greatbelonda, and they were that Gheghedo becomes a gardener's apprentice to help the aging head gardener Flowerdale. Next offer to Reah was that she becomes a trainee alongside Grasylee AKA Suemo in the kitchen.

All meals found, and new clothes shall be bought; both were something that the two, now ex-sweeps, had never known nor even dreamt of. Reah and Gheghedo excitedly accepted these extraordinary offers and thanked the kind, compassionate and considerate Lady Greatbelonda. A better night's sleep would be enjoyed by the youngsters, and it was truly both, a day to forget and also, at the same time, remember.

The small box showing magical signs.

It was from that night's sleep that Jonathan woke up and opened his eyes to the all too familiar surroundings of dense woodland and his sanctuary of the shopping trolley. It took Jonathan a while to accustom himself to something other than black chimneys. Thoughts that passed through his mind of the things experienced were compared to the threat of bullies and decided that the lesser of the two evils is the life he lives now. It just goes to show that there is always something worse, there are always people worse off than yourself; this does not mean that bullies are acceptable (it should never be) or that they should be endured (it should never be).

Jonathan recalls the last moment he saw any part of Tapeloc, and that was the memory of two small feet appearing to dance a jig as they disappeared never to be seen dancing again, and because of that, the song/jig would be renamed 'Tapeloc's Jig'. To any of the readers who feel inclined to 'play the tune', 'sing the song' or 'dance the jig', Jonathan asks that before they do, a toast is offered in the memory of the poor young 'sweep' Tapeloc.

Chapter 2
The Riddle of the Medicine Wheel

Players: Percus, Dowerdo, Penijur, Prycess, Hebec, Erios, Olinagma, Thunkbroc, Lemtry, Raplop, Thutscen, Vengamor, Lawtun.

It is from this first adventure that Jonathan became a little more aware of the difference between friends and close friends. Not that Jonathan had any, that we would call, close friends, but that transpired when some new pupils arrived at the school, and a chance meeting took place when the tallest of the newcomers tripped over a nearby tree root, and Jonathan helped the unfortunate person to his feet. This tall pupil had also been carrying a couple of books which Jonathan retrieved from the undergrowth; one of which was a book of ancient history; this was an almost unbelievable coincidence (this was also Jonathan's favourite subject) and the beginning of the makings of a 'close' friend. To put icing on the cake, Jonathan's new friend looked like a rugby player in the making, and their mutual interest in history helped to bond this friendship. The size of this new friend actually acted as a deterrent to unwanted bullying, but only whilst Jonathan and his friend were together; but after constant bullying, any respite was indeed great news. Jonathan has learnt from this adventure the value of a close and true friend and, of course, the effort, sacrifice and loyalty that must be forthcoming from both parties to cement such a friendship. Everyone will experience a number of these so-called coincidences during their lifetime; the secret is how to react and take advantage of the oft hidden purpose of these, sometimes obvious but equally sometimes vague, coincidences. Ask yourself, why has this happened? What could possibly be the purpose? Will it be to 'your' advantage or to help someone else?

The new pupil trips, and the books go flying.

In many cases the outcome is not immediately obvious but may become so at a later date; this is called an 'A, HA' moment.

This particular day, the sun was shining, the light breeze whispered through the trees creating the most pleasant rustling sound which acted as a backdrop for the melodious singing of birds; a day of dreams, a day to dream, a day to enjoy, a day that stirs the senses, every one of them.

Senses, now there's a thing, *'what are they,'* I thought, *'where do they come from and what are they for? If only I knew, could they help me? Well, perhaps they will one day, some day, maybe.'*

The bullies had chased Jonathan's friends; he recalls that he was isolated and sad, and that there is nothing wrong with him, he is just small that's all and can just watch others enjoy togetherness and fun and just see the smiles on their faces; there must be an answer, surely. Trouble is they (the bullies) live near him, and it's a little difficult to escape their influence, especially when their pastime and hobby appears to be to bully others, and they seem to take pleasure seeing someone suffer, not only physically but mentally too.

Hey-ho, Jonathan smiles at this day. It's not a school day; although, he does enjoy learning, some days should be for play, pastimes and friends; his friends this day are the trees, animals and birds; his pastime is learning their ways, and his play is with them. To think that a tree could be a friend, could be seen as a little foolish, but just because something stays in one place does not mean it can't experience life, emotion and spiritual awareness. There is definitely a physical presence. But, can there be communication? Well, just maybe there can. One of Jonathan's most favourite of trees is a large Ash, a tree that he had read the Anglo-Saxons favoured for making tools and utensils, a resilient and easily worked wood. Jonathan had climbed to the lower branches of this tree where he could listen to the 'real world', a world of insects, animals, birds and plants. Above, there sings a song thrush and a warbler; close by, there is a buzz of a large bumblebee, and below, about thirty yards away, a fallow deer nibbles at the lower branches of a thorn bush. This is peace. This is life. This is smiling time, and he feels a sense of gratitude to be able to experience such things.

Jonathan recalls the sound of a snapping twig, and that the deer suddenly stops feeding on the succulent new shoots, tilts its head and with one almighty leap is gone from sight. The birds abruptly cease their melodies, and Jonathan suddenly realised that something was afoot. He quickly descends from the tree and catches sight of the two bullies, and using the speed developed from running around his morning paper round, he heads for his refuge, the shopping trolley. The refuge is well-hidden in the undergrowth, and Jonathan curls up as quiet as a harvest mouse and settles nervously, even shaking slightly, listens to the occasional cracking and rustling slowly becoming more distant, but daring not to move, Jonathan drifts (not actually into sleep) but into another time and another place.

There is a great rumbling. It sounds louder than thunder, and the ground is shaking beneath his feet. He opens his eyes to find himself looking down from a small hill at what seems like a sea consisting of millions upon millions of buffaloes, also known as bison. These beasts are travelling south across wide open plains dotted with woodlands and dissected by sparkling streams. Jonathan is now known as Dowerdo, a native of the vast continent of North America in a time long ago; as a matter of fact, there were no signs of cars, railroads, buildings or even roads, just wide open space occupied by animals, trees, grass and bees. Nowhere to be seen are mobile phones, televisions or computers; this is a world without electricity, not even a horse; literally, a world of nature and awareness.

Jonathan imparts to me that as soon as he is in another time, another place, the world around him is fully recognisable, and all the people around him are known to him, and they know of him. After spying on the seemingly never-ending migrating bison, Dowerdo had spent enough time watching the great herd pass by; it will take another three weeks before the vast multitude shows any signs of slowing down, and although a wondrous sight, one can only watch so many animals.

The startled deer leaps to freedom.

His three younger brothers Penijur, Hebec and Lemtry made their way back to the woodland glade, a large clearing beside the stream of fresh water flowing straight from the slopes of the Rocky Mountains. In single file the quartet wound their way downhill from their vantage point reaching the campsite exchanging greetings and smiles with everyone they met. Circular tepees spread out before them, and there in distance, could be seen their mother Olinagma weaving cloth outside the home. Their father, Thunkbroc, is still away from the camp with the rest of the braves, ensuring an ample supply of fresh meat, skins and horn; all essential, not only to the wellbeing but also the survival of the whole settlement.

The great herd of Bison thunder across the prairie.

There were chores to do before the younger members of the tribe could play games; chores that were a way of life and not at all tedious but quite enjoyable (all chores should be completed with a smile and sense of purpose). These included: wood gathering for the fires, cleaning areas around the tepees and carrying the animal hide bags of water from the mountain stream which flowed nearby. That done, a group of around twenty youngsters gathered around an ancient carved stone on the edge of the village, a stone which stood just over a yard in height and displaying rows of horizontal lines dissected by small groups, at intervals of vertical cuts; some say that they belonged to a lost language of ancient travellers. This is where the younger members of the village hold mock discussions (copying the adults who hold great talks in one of the larger tepees every full moon) which acted as a platform for solving of problems or development of new ideas as well as setting of rules, ethics; in other words, 'moral codes' which were, not exactly a type of religion but actually 'a way of life'; a guide acting as a path to follow. Erios, who seemed to have the gift of the tongue, opened the meeting (just like the adults of the tribe) with greetings to all there and asked if there were any problems. Instead of every person shouting out at the same time, there was a protocol, and it was up to the person to the immediate left of Erios to speak and then, in turn, following to the left until no one was left unheard. The same procedure was followed with any answers or suggestions to the question asked until all issues were solved.

Sometimes, the adult meetings went on for many hours if not days; it was good that these meetings began only with a full moon; unless, of course, something required immediate action. The practice of sitting in a circle is lost in time, but it is, without exception, one of the most powerful shapes in the universe; a circle cannot function correctly without all its components, which actually depends on why the circle is being used. In this tribe, the format for a moon meeting requires the circle to be split into four sections occupying the cardinal points, each containing ten people. The first section being the seating place for the most enlightened to the physical world; likely to be composed of the hunters, farmers, and those most aware of the impact of any alterations to the land and the creatures that dwell thereon.

The ancient stone displaying mysterious writing.

This first group is one of the most important to people who rely on the land and nature for survival. The second segment would be occupied by the ten most mentally powerful. This would add rational perception to the discussion. The third segment is reserved for the ten most spiritually motivated tribal members; these are the people who understand the needs of not only the members of the tribe but also the psychic or mystical requirements of the land and all that roams and grows on it. In the final segment is a gathering of the ten most emotional people which will add passion and purpose to any argument. As a group, the total members would translate as the 'will of the people'; these could be called the judges as they are the ones who decide the solutions, the verdicts and the actions; but only after listening to all the arguments. In other tribes, these circles were known as 'medicine wheels', not only because they were used to heal but also offered a place within to meet and solve problems, and that the word medicine was not always used in a modern medical sense but rather meant something that could provide a solution to a problem, whether it be physical, spiritual or logical.

The young ones would mirror the actions of the 'moon meeting' but supply only four people to a segment, although, even with one person to each segment, as long as they possess the correct skill or trait, the answers and decisions will or should be the correct outcome. Jonathan looks forward to giving this a try in the modern world which does seem to be an excellent idea as each segment adds a contribution culminating in the most agreeable and acceptable solution. Remembering that to all problems there is a key which opens the door to an action to take; if the action is ignored, the problem will stay and fester upon the mind blocking the passage to harmony. Jonathan is already talking about ways to solve his problems and will follow the guidelines of the 'moon meetings' but, because of the number of people required, he himself will act out all the groups putting on different hats, as it were and see what comes from that. Although it would, in fact, be the thoughts and suggestions of one person, which is far from the ideal, the answer may transpire, but it could be a little self-opinionated. Of course, a preference of more people would, no doubt, give a better balanced argument but let's see what happens; I wished Jonathan good luck with that.

There were a few minor problems which came to light as Erios listened; the first being the issue of the missing moccasins of Percus and next the matter concerning Vengamor, the eldest son of the eldest son of Chief Raplop, who is complaining of having to work a lot more than any of the other young ones with little time to play. Concerning the moccasins made by Percus apparently, one of the girls of the village had disappeared from the front of her tepee a week ago, and the moccasins had been seen on the feet of a young brave (to be) who was actually wearing them at the meeting. The young brave, who had been identified as none other than Thutscen, claimed ownership and that the moccasins belonged to him as he had made them not long ago, and unfortunately, no one had seen Percus make them, her first self-made moccasins. There may be a little sadness, having made something that disappeared without the use or pleasure of wearing. After discussing the issue, it was revealed that there is no evidence that the maker could be identified so the owner at the moment, so thought Erios, could keep the shoes. It was at this moment that Dowerdo, after a little thought, spoke out with a suggestion to the problem; he asked for two squares of leather, each big enough to make a single shoe and suggested that the answer would soon come when a task is set for both parties to make a pair of moccasins, right there, right now, in front of the whole circle. It took no time at all to see that Thutscen was absolutely hopeless at sewing anything and was forced to admit that he picked up the moccasins thinking that they had been abandoned and admitted that the moccasins, which Percus had just made, matched perfectly to the to the pair on his feet. Thutscen admitted that he had been foolish, and that he was envious of the quality of the shoes and could only offer his apology. Taking off the moccasins, he handed them back to Percus and asked for his shame to be forgiven; Percus, in return, handed back the moccasins to Thutscen as a gift, and that it would please her to see someone enjoy the items that she had crafted, and that her skill belongs to the village and not to her alone. This shows that many things can come from one thoughtless act, but a little thought before the act can save a lot of unwanted aftereffects; but most of all, the 'medicine wheel' of the moon meeting again found the path to follow. Now came the turn of Vengamor, who was more than unhappy with all the extra work he was expected to do, but it did become a little clearer when the members of the medicine circle discussed the situation. Many of them spoke of the responsibilities of his father, Raplop, the chief of this tribe, and it was because of this that his son, who will one day become chief, must work and learn over and above the 'ordinary' braves of the village. Erios heard a number of arguments most relating to the fact that everyone knew young Vengamor was set more tasks than the rest, but what to do to help the situation. Erios offered to the members of the wheel that the future of the tribe depended great deal on the strength and wisdom of the chief; meaning that the next leader of the tribe must learn the ways of 'life and land' so that the members of the tribe can look at the chief for correct guidance. Discussion was mainly from sections two and four offering consoling words of truth, which seemed, on the surface, like extra work but was, in fact, an essential part of this process, and therefore, Vengamor must have the fortitude to accept the challenge. (Jonathan recalls that there was a look of weariness in the eyes of Vengamor, who bowed his head slightly as if under an invisible weight, the weight of responsibility). At this moment, Hebec, who had spoken with Dowerdo and others in the fourth segment of the circle, gives a cough, a clearing of throat, and stands upright and tall within the circle; there is a pause and obvious silence in anticipation of wise words from the judge's portion yet unspoken. Agreeing with Herios that a pending chief should have instruction on all the knowledge required for the survival of the tribe, and that Vengamor must shoulder the burden and also the realisation of the commitment required, but maybe not alone. What is suggested by this segment is that the burden is not shouldered alone, and that the general chores could be shared amongst the members gathered here in the 'medicine wheel', therefore, leaving Vengamor to concentrate on learning the ways of leadership and hence, giving him a little more time to relax and play; both of which are also essential parts of life's development of mind and body. You could see a sudden change in Vengamor, a twinkle in his eye, a smile on his lips as he thanked the 'medicine wheel' for providing the key and is looking forward to the help that is offered.

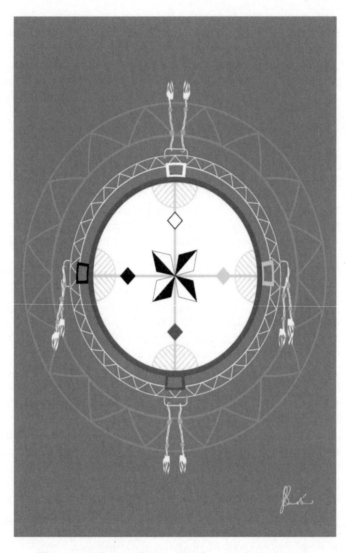

The powerful medicine wheel, a symbol of truth.

This is the benefit of collective thinking, collective action and the acceptance, indeed, of the saying, 'many hands make light work' as well as the future value of a tribe that works together to support the chief. There were nods of approval for both solutions for the problems presented that day and a certain recognition that the 'younger' tribal members did more than justice to their interpretation of the adult medicine wheel.

It was now time for thoughts of food as the hunters returned with a bounty of fruits and meat from a more than successful day. These goods were carried on 'A'-frames dragged by the stronger braves, made lighter by the many songs sung on the way back; as they entered the camp, there could be heard 'wo yay yay wo' a haunting rendition called the song of the coyote. The rhythm of this particular song, set by the rattles of the braves, actually mimics the walking pace of the frame carriers, and what a wonderful sound echoing through the glade. Jonathan likened it to the sounds of nature accompanied by the chanting spirits of the ancestors. Everyone joined in as if the whole world was singing; everyone greeting the hunters; everyone helping to unload and either store or prepare the food. This was the first great hunt of the season, and there would be a great feast to celebrate a successful hunt and thank to the buffalo for coming by. After the feast, the adult medicine wheel would be formed, and more serious business presented; younger members of the tribe usually 'listened in' from distance so as not to interrupt the proceedings but still learn techniques from their elders. The meeting is set for the elder folk, now that the hunters have returned and with them some strangers from a tribe named Micmac came to speak at the moon meeting; drums could be heard which signalled all the participants to gather and form the medicine wheel. The proceedings began with the passing of the pipe of peace showing all those present that the thoughts were peaceful and the palms empty of weapons, but the minds open to debate. There were a few minor problems concerning the sharing of the proceeds of the hunt (equal to all was the outcome) and the seating order at the funeral of the relatives of one of the braves who was, unfortunately, killed by stampeding buffalo (soon sorted with preference given to the relatives of the brave over the relatives of his squaw). Now stands the spokesperson of the Micmac tribe, a tall brave, known as Lawtun, whose face showed the lines of many journeys, and eyes that hid many tales and only truth comes from his lips.

With power in voice, Lawtun explained that most of the tribe had been displaced by more powerful tribes forcing them to abandon good country in the North-West and after many moons walk through lands unknown across many steep mountains and fast flowing waters, they arrived on flat plains bountiful of animals and plants. The people of the Micmac are weary and only number fifty-three, all that is left of the tribe, and there is a need to settle at the end of the journey; to build wigwams and grow and prosper, but they lack skills. They are hunters, fishers, gatherers, and people of the forest and the sea-shores who seek the guidance and expertise of the plains tribes. They have come to this village in peace with open hand and heart to speak in the 'medicine wheel' of the moon. They had great knowledge of making flint tools, a knowledge obtained from the northern tribes, and Lawtun called upon his squaw Prycess, who pulled from her bag the most magnificent 'Clovis' blade ever seen and handed it over to the chief Raplop who walked the circle showing this great work of functioning art, a treasure indeed. Lawtun explained that his small band was but a splinter of a once great tribal tree, and that he had no knowledge of the fate or whereabouts of the rest of the Micmac and feared that this fragments were the only survivors. Prycess, who had been attending to the five children of the group offered another great gift; during the sharing of the feast, she had noticed the large stone, around which Dowerdo and the other juveniles had held their own meeting. Prycess explained that many, many seasons, in fact, lifetimes ago, the Micmac were visited by great boats from the sea, mastered by mysterious people who worshipped strange gods and wrote stories which they carved on stone for the benefit of the tribes; the meanings of which were lost in time but for a few. The lines upon the stone in this village are almost the same and could be read by Prycess (a skill obtained from an elder of the tribe Micmac). These are the skills that the Micmac can offer, training in the art of fighting so that they can protect their hunting grounds and valuable information as yet unlocked from the written symbols etched into the ancient monolith. Around the medicine wheel discussions began, and the first question was 'do we need the skills of fighting?' As there are no enemies, such a skill is of little use, although, the skill may be of use in the future but time spent on training would have to be matched by time spent on constant practice. The decision was to decline the offer of the fighting skills, but keep the offer open for the future. The Micmac required land to farm, and the tribe to which Dowerdo belonged had more land than was needed at the moment, and it was agreed that the Micmac could farm the land on the pretext that they gave a quarter of the harvest each season to the chief Raplop to distribute amongst his tribe. Lawtun agreed to this and was happy at the outcome. Prycess, in the meantime, had been studying the inscriptions on the ancient stones which had turned out to be instructions for the production of bronze. This is a mystery to the tribe of Raplop because the use of metals are unknown to these people but the advantages are multiple, and with the interpretation as a guide, this is a possible bargaining tool. Discussion amongst the 'medicine wheel' by the elders showed that are certain advantages, such as; stronger axes for felling trees for firewood and longer lasting pots for cooking. Dowerdo and the young members of the tribe had heard all this from their vantage point and were intrigued by the possibility of uncovering the mysteries of ancient travellers who had arrived by sea. *'But why,'* they thought, *'was this writing on a stone so many miles from the ocean?'* Not one of the youngsters had even seen the ocean and only knew of its existence from tales told after meal times, of golden lands washed by great waves of never-ending blue seas. The watchers were dropping off to sleep after a long day of activity; a good day, a day to remember, a day not to be forgotten. It was decided to leave two or three of the watchers to listen to the rest of the debate and so report back to the group the following morning, and chosen were Hebec, Percus and Lemtry; at least the majority will have a good night's rest before the work of the next day begins.

The day began with an update from the 'medicine wheel', and all were told by Lemtry that little happened after the young one had left. As agreed in their own 'medicine wheel', the younger ones shared the chores of Vengamor as well as their own, which included the gathering of herbs, seeds and fruits, enough for the day and firewood for the cooks, and as everyone mucked in, it was not a hard task, and the woodland echoed with songs.

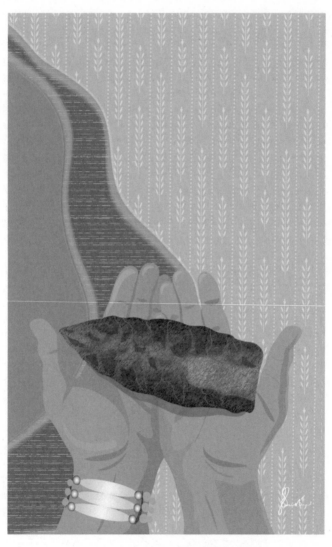

The presentation of a Clovis blade.

This was a good life as there were no enemies, only nature to contend with, and nature was kind, the climate warm, and a cool breeze blew every day from mid-morning to mid-afternoon.

Jonathan, sitting opposite me, whilst I write this down, closes his eyes as if he was feeling the warmth of the sun and hearing the songs of the gatherers; his smile was one to behold almost ear to ear. Is this a reality that I write from the words of Jonathan, or was it all a dream? Is life a dream? Are there many lives that we live side by side when the vast majority of us only know one, and a chosen few can venture to these past and future times? I discussed with Jonathan the aspects and possibilities of how this could be conceivable and came up with the idea of the 'butterfly effect', as if a person was the body of a butterfly, and the wings were tendrils to these other worlds; this is best seen from the illustration below. From the wings of the butterfly, it is possible to have a memory from either the future or a memory of the past, and experience, either in 'now' or in different dimensions. That is why someone might say "I've had a premonition" or "I knew that would happen"; all they are doing is homing in on events that have actually happened but are in the future to someone in 'the now'. Jonathan is lucky enough to have a 'connection' to all the lives he has or is due to live; a phenomenon experienced up to the age of two or three years, and then the human brain normally cuts the connection. Now that the reader is enlightened, let us go back to the recollections of Jonathan.

Apparently, other stones had been found nearby but had spent years lying flat, and the writing on them almost worn away, but it became obvious, with the help of Prycess, that the whole process from making a kiln to mould production was there to be seen. As the tribe of Raplop had no knowledge of writing (they had only the spoken word), the stones were nothing more than 'something from the past'. (The writing has both a close resemblance to that of 'Linear A', a precursor of writing known as 'Linear B' which gives an origin from none other than ancient Greece and particularly the islands of Cyprus and Crete and that of a form from the ancient Phoenicians). These seafaring people of long ago who came in ships were not only warriors but great teachers too, and there appears to be more than one type of writing, and as Prycess argues, there may have been more than one lot of visitors many years apart.

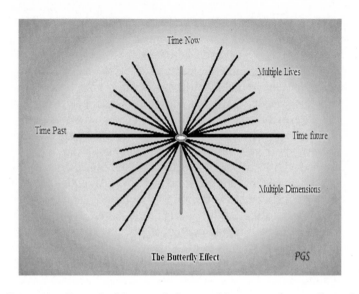

Prycess only reads the curved signs and has no understanding of the straight lines found on only one of these stones. Dowerdo was quick to assist Prycess and became a star pupil and actually the first person from the tribe of Raplop to read any sort of language. Below are some of the letters that were found on the stones in and around the village, as remembered by Dowerdo.

The Micmac sent out scouts to find the ores (the raw materials) needed to make the bronze axes and soon came across the more abundant requirement which was copper, but it did take another four days to locate tin; these are the two most popular mixes that when melted would become bronze. All the tribe were excited with this newfound knowledge, and rather than try and construct a large furnace, Lawtun suggested that each tepee should make their very own small 'pit' furnace. The scouts retuned with many bags of copper ore, ready crushed where they had found a rich deposit; it now looked like small green flakes. Everyone was ready at their small bucket-sized pits, kindling and dry grass at the bottom then charcoal with the crushed ore and set alight. A clay air tube inserted to blow in more air and all covered to seal in the heat; some used tube to blow in the air, and others used bellows constructed from animal skins, a method which proved more effective. It was not long before great temperatures were reaching over 900 centigrade, and the ore turned to liquid and dripped to the bottom of the furnace and solidified on cooling. This gave everyone a handful of copper, which the Micmac tribe gathered up; the same happened with the tin ore, and then everything was pounded again and mixed nine parts copper to one part tin, put into small crucibles back in the furnaces. Moulds were made in two halves out of stone bound together, and the resulting mixed liquid metal was poured into the moulds and left to set. There must have been twenty of these moulds, all ready to be opened, and the whole village gathered to watch and were amazed when out popped shiny yellow axe heads which the Micmac people cleaned and sharpened and presented to chief Raplop. There were woops, singing and great joy for all as they marvelled at this new craft.

Dowerdo along with Prycess and Erios uncovered two more of the writing stones and noticed a carving on one of them; a carving of something never seen before. It was circular with what appeared to be an arrow through it with lettering below. It was at this point that Erios suggested that they copy this mysterious object and make a mould for it; all three agreed. Erios volunteered to make the mould, Dowerdo offered to collect the green-coloured stone, and Prycess undertook to make the small furnace. So, off they went in different directions. Later that day, they met again when Erios produced a beautifully crafted stone mould which he had chipped away using fine flint sherds. Prycess had the small furnace prepared with kindling and charcoal, and a crucible, she had made from an old cooking pot, and Dowerdo produced a handful of coloured stones but not green copper producing ore, more of a yellow colour.

Apparently, the copper mine was too dangerous, so he had picked up these yellow chunks instead; no problem, as the three agreed to use those instead. The fire is lit, the charcoal is glowing, the air pipe in place and the chunks are in the crucible, now to cover the furnace and pump the bellows. Jonathan chuckled as he remembers that they had been pumping for half an hour, and the chunks had not melted.

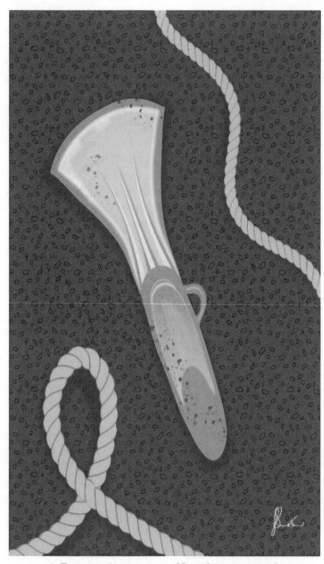

A Bronze-Age axe; a gift to be treasured.

So they inserted another air pipe and pumped harder until, at last, the chunks had started to melt; the temperature was a lot hotter than needed for the copper. Into the mould, the yellow liquid went, and the three waited for a while for it to cool down, and it was not until the breaking of the mould took place that the object was gazed upon. What a wondrous thing was before them, gleaming, shining and as yellow as the sun itself. Prycess had added four dark red stones she had removed from her necklace and inserted into to this jewel, copying the style carved upon the large stone. They showed this thing of beauty to the chief Raplop who had never seen the like, and the Micmac leader Lawtun, who had heard tales of this metal from travellers from lands many moons to the south, who believed it to be tears of the sun. To which, Dowerdo added that there were many more chunks just laying by the stream which ran down by the rocky cliffs, just a short walk away from where the copper ore was found. Just a few days ago, this tribe had no knowledge of either metal working or writing, but with the help of the people of the Micmac, the tribe of chief Raplop were literally mesmerised, and people talked about nothing else for many moons. It was not long before they were making little models of people, animals and trees from these metals, and the flint blades that they used are almost forgotten.

Jonathan has no further memories of these people, but now has the knowledge that strangers can be helpful and an asset to the community and has little doubt that these two groups, hence, lived in harmony. Neither group made the mistake of trying to force their own ways on each other, and like the copper and tin amalgamated into one; not only living side-by-side but amongst and within. Jonathan tells me that he still has memories of the strange writing which he can now read and understand (much to the amazement of his history teacher, Mrs. McGowan). Jonathan reflects upon the reality that he was in this strange land for many weeks, but climbing from the shopping trolley, he realised that an hour had passed, in here and now. The only thing that he can bring back from these travelling is the memory, and with the knowledge gained as a result, he can find ways to overcome the difficulties of being the victim of bullies. Things like the advantages of discussion as a way of finding an amicable solution; as both the youngsters and the elders of the tribes found out: if it works, use it. Thank goodness for the trolley, thank goodness for the gift of travel; even though, it appears to be all in the mind, or is it? Listening to these tales, they sound convincing to me, and indeed, how else could Jonathan have learnt to read an ancient language but from being there, somewhere in the Americas?

The 'Jewel' in all its glory.

The coast was clear, and Jonathan made a run for home. There are not many people that can run faster than him now; a talent he learnt which helps escape, and there is no harm in that, is there? With this tale in mind, you can say that that's another 'arrow in his belt'; pardon the pun. The next tale or actually adventure Jonathan reveals to me is where he meets his first real love and learns the words of love. I look forward to this and have sharpened my pencils, opened my jotter in readiness and with eagerness arrange the next meeting time. By the way, I am the pupil who tripped and fell, and now Jonathan and I are 'best friends'. I'll have you know, friends that last a lifetime, friends that you should never ignore. They are few and far between, believe me.

Chapter 3
The Moon Dances upon the Seine

Players: Poglerbea, Katse, Pidlarch, Rotut Monlas, Raggynil, Kepi, Ebblar, Goguden, Lumtel, Harco.

It is the start of a new term, and Jonathan is on his usual walk to school. Near the entrance gates, he spots the bullies, and they are there to cause trouble, so Jonathan takes a side step and heads for the playing fields; he knows he can outrun these guys. They make little effort to try and catch him, as the bullies are well aware that they will be left behind as Jonathan crosses the playing fields to enter the school through the back gates. Jonathan is warned by one of the bullies that they will be waiting for him when the school finishes, so he devises a scheme to be working late, which actually involves talking during classes. This works well in the maths class when Jonathan constantly talks to other pupils resulting in him being kept behind for detention: writing five hundred lines of 'I must not talk in class'. A thankless task, but it takes just over an hour to finish the punishment, and with a furtive look outside the school doors, Jonathan starts for home. Going around the first corner, he is confronted by two of the bullies so he turns to run, but unknown to him, there are two more behind him; now that is not good; they must have sussed out his ruse and lay in wait. He is grabbed and held tight, then they snatch his satchel and remove his books and note pads and have great delight in tearing out the pages and piling them up. What followed is just downright wickedness, as one of the bullies, with a cigarette lighter in his hand, sets fire to the pages (these books were Jonathan's favourite reading books); not only the books go up in smoke, but also his notebooks are put on the pile; much to the amusement of the bullies. They also take his shoe laces and pocket money but are very careful not to leave any bruises which, I suppose, is a blessing in disguise, and they finish by rubbing the ashes all over his face and clothes. After taking a few snaps of Jonathan, who is looking all the worse for the experience, the bullies satisfied and laughing warn Jonathan not to say anything or else. What the reason is for doing this is not hard to understand as there are similarities in the animal kingdom as a form of dominance strategy and as an indication of signifying that they are the rulers. On reflection, Jonathan has suggested that this is, in fact, a form of collective cruelty not often seen as an animal trait; unfortunately, some people have an overdeveloped mean streak. I see watering in the eyes of Jonathan as he recalls that once again he heads for the wooded area and the all too familiar shopping trolley; on his way, he washes the dark stains of ash from his face, in the brook next to the wood and curls up like a ball inside the trolley wondering where or what comes next and drift off. At times, I wish I could have done more to protect him, but it is not practical, and I cannot be there as a guard twenty-four seven.

There is music, laughter, the clinking of wine glasses as Jonathan tells me about the next adventure; his name is now Pidlarch, and he is somewhere in Paris, in a café near the banks of the river Seine. This is a happy time, a time of self-expression, enjoyment, learning, drinking and song; all around the walls of the café are paintings for sale, small ones, big ones, beautiful and ugly ones. The table on which Pidlarch places his wine is home to a small well-knit group of friends. Sat to the left is Poglerbea (probably the oldest of the group who acts as a father figure), a flamboyant artist, always covered in specks of paint, almost a walking canvas whose livelihood stems from the painting of portraits. Across the table can be found Raggynil, dressed in a plain blouse but wearing a skirt of many colours and a wide bonnet to match; she is a talented cellist who is lucky enough to play in one of the most famous Parisian orchestras and plays the accordion not for money but just for enjoyment. To the right is Kepi who is the daughter of an aristocrat, everyone knows that is not her real name, and a person who seems to take pleasure by mingling with the artisans. No one seems to mind as she, although in her late teens, has no hesitation at all in splashing a few francs about, but this seems to attract leeches and hangers-on. Next around the table tonight is Ebblar, an author and playwright in the making, who is practicing his speech for his

21st birthday party tomorrow. Ebblar's most famous and oft repeated boast is that of having spoken to none other than Victor Hugo (a famous novelist and poet before Victor Hugo moved to Guernsey), who had plans to publish a book called *'Les Miserables'* and not only spoken to but had actually read the manuscript of Hugo. No doubt, there will be others joining and leaving the group during the evening, but as Raggynil flexes the accordion, a lively tune filled the air. Tonight she starts with a *Bal-musette* rendition that gets the majority onto their feet, and Pidlarch takes advantage of an empty seat, but no sooner that he relaxes into the comfort of the chair, his arm is grabbed by Kepi, and they twirl on the dance area, until breathless. What great fun had by all until the hours call a halt, and the reality of tiredness takes hold, and most of the group departs into the night when Pidlarch enjoys the refreshing air on his short walk by the Seine back to the comfort of his small but cosy lodgings. After a day of writing, Pidlarch (apparently a budding scribe, a writer of poems and plays) is looking forward to the birthday party of Ebblar and the company of many friends. In collaboration with others, Pidlarch had produced a sketch for a short comedy with music, centred upon the style and traits of Ebblar and in doing so, had arrived early at the café upon the banks of the Seine. Poglerbea appears shortly after and smartly dressed for once, in readiness to play the part of Victor Hugo beard and all. Not long to go before the birthday boy arrives, but there is someone missing; the player who was to take the part of 'Adèle'; the wife of Hugo had not turned up and panic starts to creep in, but the sketch could still be performed without her. Raggynil, who was to supply the background music, thought she could save the day and introduces Katse, a relative of hers staying in Paris for a few weeks and was convinced Katse could be an excellent stand in. The skit went well with Poglerbea reading out excerpts of both Hugo's early poetry and the *'Hunchback of Notre Dame'* and entering into conversation with Katse playing a superb 'Adèle', who was notorious because of her apparent lack of interest in anything to do with the 'arts' which had everyone in laughter. Pidlarch mentioned that he was taken with the softness of the voice of Katse, and indeed, there was more than a glimmer or perhaps a sparkle in the eye of Katse as she glanced in the direction of Pidlarch as he read a short poem celebrating the party. It was now time for Raggynil to play her most famous of renditions of *La Toupie* in the style of *Bal-musette.* Pidlarch approached the young Katse and offered an outstretched hand as an invitation to accept him as partner for this fast, exciting, at times, intimate traditional dance. I could see in the eyes of Jonathan as he recollects that first dance that this could be a classic case of 'love at first sight'. Never before had he felt like this, and it was definitely not the wine that resulted in a feeling of euphoria; a happiness beyond happiness, and they danced and danced until exhaustion. Escorting each other back to the table, gasping for breath, a sparkling wine was called for, and it could be seen that, as they sat side by side, they were oblivious of the surroundings with their hands clasped and eyes on no one but themselves. A rest from dance music brought into the limelight two operatic singers, the beautiful Lumtel with flowing locks and colourful garments sporting her favourite red shoes and the moustachioed Harco, one of the best tenors seen on any stage this side of the Alps and always a welcome patriot of the café. Both the singers enjoyed the challenge of a chance to indulge in 'native' music at its roots.

They are joined by Ebblar because it was his party, forming a trio leading the now packed crowd in various renditions of some popular folk songs of the day, accompanied by the effervescent Raggynil on the well-used accordion. Everyone joined in, resulting in a sound reminiscent of a hundred seals at twilight accompanied by a flock of anxious gulls, and it was definitely no choir but fantastic enjoyment. There was dancing and merriment into the early hours before people began to drift away, and Raggynil felt much like a gooseberry as she informed Katse that it was time to leave and say her goodbyes. Pidlarch had hoped for more time with his newly found friend but after a mutually excepted kiss, wished both a pleasant evening and on departing conveyed his request to Katse that they meet again; an offer that was accepted with little hesitation.

Loving hands meet across the table.

During the days following the party, Pidlarch talked at length with Poglerbea explaining the feelings he had for Katse and how overwhelmed with emotions his mind had become. Being a long-lived and well-travelled individual, Poglerbea could offer both advice and caution to young Pidlarch about the affairs of heart. The main guidance was towards keeping ones feet firmly on the ground in the first encounters as this will give time to evaluate the situation and develop a strategy geared to a more flexible manoeuvrability. Poglerbea suggested that 'the heart' be kept safe, for now at least, inside an outer ring of doubt and care; this will act as a safeguard against the perils of disappointment, failure and heartache which can have devastating consequences. Then again, what could be called true love could happen but once or twice during a lifetime, and the opportunity to experience such must not be missed. So in a nutshell, the advice given by Poglerbea, in essence, suggested that the victim follows their heart but with a little caution, if at all possible. Pidlarch pondered the words of wisdom and decided that because of the feelings he already has for Katse, he will transmit his thoughts into a poem to Katse and accept the outcome; at least he would find out at this early stage so as to protect his heart, just as Poglerbea suggested. It took no more than ten minutes to pen the poem which reflected his mood and is actually a rather forward romantic approach with, as Pidlarch thought, a 'nothing to lose' exercise. The title *'Mine Heart As If Is Yours'* leaves little to the imagination and is concise, direct and meaningful; or so thought Pidlarch.

He seals the poem inside an envelope and on his next meeting with Raggynil passes the item over and asks the favour of handing it to, her charge, Katse. Promisingly, Raggynil tells Pidlarch that Katse had talked of nothing else than the party of Ebblar and the handsome Pidlarch and would take pleasure to carry out that small task. It was not until seven days had passed that Pidlarch heard from Katse in the form of a written reply. In the letter, there was an indication that Katse would be thrilled to join Pidlarch for lunch and an apology for the time lapse, but that she had been away from Paris. Pidlarch could be seen that afternoon walking by the riverside almost waltzing with a pronounced spring in his step; this, indeed, is a sign of the power of love, as an aphrodisiac of the mind.

Mine Heart as If Is Yours

Wouldst a cloud, not cross the sky
Without, a thought of you
Wouldst a hound, not bark
Without, your voice be heard

Ever a drop of rain but fall, upon my head
That as if, I touch your hand
Ever a drop of wine, be sipped
That as if, our lips would meet

If our eyes, do together gaze
Mine heart, as if is yóurs
If your smile, does glow with love
Mine tears, do clog my lash

Whilst the earth endlessly rotates
We hold the key
Whilst our souls combined above
We hold the truth

Forever as one, to ride the stars
In peace and fondness true
Forever as one, in mind entwined
In harmony and accord.

Raggynil arranged the meeting which would be in two days'
time at the café where they all met, but first Raggynil was keen
to talk to Pidlarch before that took place; this would take place
this very evening. Just after sunset, after a busy day, Pidlarch
looked forward to his evening with friends but was wondering
why Raggynil wanted to talk; perhaps, she was going to offer
words of wisdom in the matters of heart. Pidlarch greets
Raggynil in their usual haunt, and over a glass of wine from the
mouth of Raggynil there flows a tale, a tale of sadness, truth and
self-sacrifice. Pidlarch sits back and listens as the life of Katse
unfolds beginning with the illness of her parents who both
succumbed to the terrible infectious disease of tuberculosis
which was sweeping across most known countries in the

nineteenth century. It was an unselfish act that Katse undertook when in her late teens she nursed and cared for both parents throughout the agonising six months culminating in their merciful depart. That in itself was hard enough to bear, but the last few months had seen Katse suffer more and more from spells of dizziness and head pain. As Raggynil went on to explain that Katse, for a little respite from caring, would ride the horse of a neighbour but unfortunately, on jumping a fence one day parted with the saddle and suffered an injury to the back of her head. It was the result of that selfless act of kindness and obligation that Katse undertook for her parents that she discounted and suffered her injuries, but now as the symptoms are increasing, and she has come to Paris to meet the eminent physician Mr Rotut Monlas who is, apparently, ready to experiment with a new procedure; they will meet tomorrow with the physician. Raggynil also explained that Katse was not ignoring Pidlarch but had just spent the whole week in the house of Raggynil until the pain was bearable enough to enjoy the outside world. Pidlarch declared that his feelings have not altered, and that his new found love was even more deeply felt. With an eagerness to meet growing every day a suggestion that a rendezvous, the day after Katse consults the eminent Monlas, be considered; this was agreed. Until then everyone went about their business, acting, singing, composing and painting; for this was an age of artistic enlightenment. Pidlarch virtually sprinted to the café, which was as usual very busy; he looked around but could not see Katse and according to others had not even arrived, so he left and sat on a wall overlooking the Seine, flicking a few small pebbles onto the mirror-like surface. An hour passed when he noticed a reflection, as if someone was looking over his shoulder; it was a reflection of loveliness and with a start jumped up and lo, and behold, there stood Katse. She stretched out her arms offering an embrace which was immediately accepted by Pidlarch; nothing was said, no words came forth, but tears could be seen slowly, like twinkling diamonds, descending the cheeks of Katse. Pidlarch suggested that they walk awhile, as the café was too busy and noisy for them to talk. The couple strolled, hand in hand, discussing the meeting between Pidlarch and Raggynil earlier that week. It was now that Pidlarch said those magic, sometimes tragic, sometimes happy words 'I love you' and held his breath for some sign that the feeling was mutual. Katse, with glee, shouted as if the world was to hear 'I love you too, forever, for always'. Pidlarch held a smile, a mile wide, until his face hurt from the elation and suggested that they go somewhere to talk alone and offered to cook her favourite meal (something he had gleaned from Raggynil), a rabbit ragout washed down with a full-bodied Cabernet Sauvignon; apparently a lot safer to drink than water of the day. With a sparkle in her eyes, Katse could not refuse such an invitation, but first, they would go to the café and inform Raggynil of their plans. The studio of Pidlarch overlooked the river, which, by the early evening, was alive with small boats and the promenade outside awash with humanity all going to their favourite haunts. Pidlarch dons his chef's hat, apron and lights the fire under the stove, being hopeful, or was it presumptive there is already on top of the stove a large pan with an equally large lid which appeared to be too large for the pan. The rabbit already skinned, chopped and flavoured with a variety of herbs, and only vegetables to dice; this is going to be an excellent meal. They sat on the aged sagging *chaise longue,* held hands, looked into each other's eyes and with a clink of glasses, toasted the day and their meeting. The meal is served, the smell of the rabbit stew filled the air with aromas so sweet accompanied by the bouquet of fresh baked bread, which invitingly laid, still warm and golden brown, next to the replenished wine glasses. Pidlarch served to his guest and received compliments on the absolutely delicious meal, especially the tenderness of the meat and exotic flavours of the rabbit. There was small talk between the two with Pidlarch waiting patiently for an opportunity to ask Katse about the outcome of her meeting with Monlas but was reluctant to bring up the subject. Katse, after more wine, appeared a little more relaxed when she actually brought up the subject herself. An operation was definitely needed as tumour had developed because of the head injury, something to do with the 'occipital lobe' which has now begun to affect her eyesight causing bouts of near blindness and pain. It transpires that the physician Rotut is willing to perform an operation to remove the suspected tumour but the only drawback was the cost of the procedure.

The table is laid and the fires lit for two lovers to share.

At this point, Katse bows her head and admits that it was beyond her budget, well beyond. Pidlarch puts a tender arm around her shoulders and holds her tight before offering reassuring words of support and understanding. This had turned out to be a rather sad evening after beginning a little more jovial two hours previous, but already Pidlarch was thinking of possible solutions to this unfortunate quandary. They were now drowning sorrows with another bottle of Sauvignon, and a little worse for this unexpected excess, it was mutually decided that Katse would stay overnight in the studio. Pidlarch gentlemanly offered his comfortable bed to Katse with the suggestion that he will sleep the night away on the *chaise longue* rather than attempt to wander through the streets in the now early hours of the morning. They kissed fondly, hugged a while, and Pidlarch cupped his hands under the chin of Katse, kissed her tenderly on her forehead, showed her to the bedroom and wished her goodnight before retiring to his lounge for the night. The next day began with the realisation that Katse faced, in the immediate future, weeks of pain and suffering but now knows that her pain is shared. It is near mid-day, and whilst Katse was still asleep Pidlarch makes his way to the café and is greeted warmly by all there. As in all tight knit communities, news travels fast, and the main question of the day was 'how is Katse'? They all knew the situation as others had noticed the ailment poor Katse was battling, and Raggynil had felt obliged to tell. Overnight Pidlarch had little sleep but had thought long and hard for a solution to the situation and came up with the idea of approaching the community at large with a plea. Up he stood with his cap in hand and from his pocket produced a small purse in which there were three gold coins each of 24 Livres (handed to him by his mother when he left for Paris four years ago; all dated 1793, they had once belonged to his grandfather); his savings, his money for a rainy day, his reserve and placed the purse and its contents in his cap and uttered these words "this is for my love; yours are for her life". There were cries of bravo, and there was soon a flow of coins from all there; some who had little to give, but they did give. Ebblar even donated what was left of his birthday funds and helped Pidlarch and Raggynil to count the generous bounty, not knowing the amount needed. All the friends could only hope that it would be enough to cover the essential operation.

Raggynil offered to go back to the studio to find out how Katse was recovering from her overindulgences and took along the now bulging hat. On returning to the café, Katse was warmly greeted by Pidlarch. Katse addressed the crowd and offered thanks to all the contributors, adding that the money would go some way towards funding the operation. Pidlarch ordered a light lunch for himself, and Katse and headed for a secluded table for two in the rear of the café. It was now that Katse grasped the hand of Pidlarch and sadly informed him that the amount of money raised is nowhere near the total required, and it appeared that there is little hope that existing funds would ever meet the cost. She was most grateful and actually a little overwhelmed with the generosity of the café goers, but now she must leave again for a few days in care of Raggynil. Katse gently kissed Pidlarch on the lips and informed him that Raggynil would be taking her to the countryside that very afternoon.

At this point, I asked Jonathan, out of curiosity, why he does not suggest more modern techniques and inventions from the 21st century, and the reply from Jonathan is indeed a little surprising (to me). Apparently, when he becomes someone in a different era, there are no memories of the persona of Jonathan, but when he returns, memories of the adventure are there in his head; vivid and bright. In a nut shell, nothing can be taken on a journey.

Back to the story, back to the café, and Pidlarch was deep in thought when Kepi came over and asked Pidlarch to fill her in with all the gossip as Kepi had been away celebrating the birth of her first niece. Pidlarch told her of the quandary of Katse for which Kepi immediately offered a solution; she would supply any shortfall between the amount raised from the hat but with one proviso 'that no one must know from whence the money came'. Kepi went on to explain that although she is never shy of paying for a round of drinks or the odd meal, she did not wish to become a target for everyone who would treat her as a 'soft touch'. Pidlarch understood and suggested the best way would be to approach surgeon Rotut Monlas directly and pay him the fee up front and of course, swear him of secrecy. It was agreed and arranged that himself and Kepi, in the next few days, will find the eminent Rotut and transact the business. There was a clang of glasses as the two of them drank a toast to the outcome of their endeavours. The meeting with Rotut went well, and he thought the whole idea was acceptable, and that there would be tight lips regarding the identity of the mysterious benefactor and also offered an ingenious suggestion to actually remove any mention of a benefactor and alleviate any awkward situations that would arise. The plan was for Rotut to tell Katse that because the procedure was still in the experimental stages, and that she would actually be a 'guinea pig', the fees would be reduced to whatever was in the hat. Unfortunately, Rotut could not forgo the fee altogether as he had bills to pay and mouths to feed but was happy to act out the façade. Pidlarch felt much happier with the outcome and retired to the studio with thoughts of Katse and most likely, she of him. It would be a few days until Katse would return so Pidlarch took that time to inform all the regulars of the café of the outcome concerning the meeting with the surgeon but not the fine details of the monetary arrangement between Kepi and Rotut. It was left up to Rotut to send the correspondence explaining the fictitious cost of the operation to Katse, and the date had been set for the following week as time was an essence. Those few days seemed like forever as Pidlarch waited for the return of Katse, but there she was waiting at the rear table were they held hands so warmly, lovingly. Katse had but one wish and that was for Pidlarch to cook what was now her favourite meal, the infamous rabbit ragout. Pidlarch retorted that nothing would give him greater pleasure and that actually his table was already set in anticipation, and it was a pleasure to be accompanied by his angel; the fire was lit in the studio and glowing with warmth and love. They walked hand in hand along the banks of the Seine with the cool evening breeze flicking the long locks of Katse dancing against the moonlight. The two had obviously missed the company of each other which showed as Pidlarch cooked the meal, Katse lent upon his shoulder and clung to him as if it were the last time they would meet. They did not eat the meal on the pre-set table but sat on the woven mat in front of the crackling fire and talked, smiled and kissed; their eyes sparkling with love; their hearts reflecting the warmth of the flames. With the meal devoured, Katse cuddled up to Pidlarch and nestled her head upon the shoulder of her love and looked tenderly into his eyes; they kiss and felt the magnetism develop and swell. For an hour, they cuddled, talked and mutually smile, contemplating the moment. Whether it was the warmth of the flames or the love in their hearts or, indeed, a combination of both, they were now in each other's arms, lost together in tender embrace. Little was said, but the pleasure was something special (as he recalls, I could see by the expression on Jonathan's face evidence that that night was indeed most memorable, and out of honour and friendship, I delve no further.) It was two days later when Raggynil came to the café carrying a hand-delivered document from Rotut which she handed over to Katse. Thinking that it contained a request for a deposit to perform the operation (for which she knew that it was something that she could never afford), Katse did not open the letter and placed it on one side and placed her hand on that of Pidlarch and looks in his eyes. A moment later, Kepi came over to ask about the health of Katse and saw the letter laying there and tactfully encourages Katse to open it whether it be good or bad. This Katse did with an air of presumption and read the letter, but all that could be seen was Katse frozen and staring in disbelief as she reads the unbelievable news. It was now that Pidlarch took the letter from the trembling hands of Katse, and both he and Raggynil did their best to look surprised at the news that Rotut will treat this as an 'experimental operation'. Kepi hugged Katse, wished her well for the good fortune and hoped that all goes well with the operation which was set for early the following week. The instructions were carefully read, and the date was set for the operation in three days' time, and although this was a moment to celebrate the good news, all could see the pain that now inflicted poor Katse. It was hugs all around; goodbye to Pidlarch, goodbye to the café, and Katse departed with Raggynil in readiness of the journey ahead. Just before they left, Pidlarch took out from his pocket a crumpled piece of paper on which was written a poem (a poem he had written a few days previous, titled 'Le Ange') and handed it to Katse and told her to read it tonight when she would be ready for bed; a kiss, goodbye but not farewell and watched as the two girls disappeared into the afternoon. Katse did exactly what she was told as she snuggled between the blankets. In the light of a flickering candle, she unfolded the sheet of paper and read the poem with tears of happiness slowly descending her cheeks, closed her eyes and fell asleep. Jonathan recalls the poem with a sadness on his brow, a smile on his lips and love in his eye. I copy the poem below for all to read.

Le Ange

If there ever was an angel
Could it be you?
If there ever was a friend
Would it be you?

I caressed your dreams
With thoughts of passion.
I caressed your hair
Bring thoughts of love.

Eager to embrace your warmth
Lapse not to your sleep.
Eager to embrace your arms
Think not to your depart.

Through the age of time we meet
Waste not the moment.
Through the age of time we live
Waste not the memory.

If there ever was an angel,
Would it be you?
If there ever was a friend,
Could it be you?

The few days passed slowly, and as far as Pidlarch was concerned, it was an eternity, but they did pass when on the morning of the operation there was knock on his studio door. On opening, he was greeted by a dozen people; there was Poglerbea, Raggynil, Kepi, Ebblar, Lumtel and Harco to name but a few. Not to forget the father of Kepi, none other than Duke Goguden, who had brought along his river boat to transport everyone to the nearest wharf not far from the surgery; friends indeed. Everyone was in good spirits; there were picnic baskets, wine and many songs sung as the boat sailed smoothly along the Seine.

I can see actual tears in the eyes of Jonathan as he recollects the most vivid memory of that early morning, when the full moon reflected in the ripples left in the boat's wake, as if the celestial body was dancing in the water reminding him of the graceful movements of his love, 'Katse', as if it was she who was dancing in those very waves. By the time the party had reached the surgery, the operation was over, and Katse was recovering but still asleep. Rotut told the party that the new procedure, for him, which involved removing a portion of the skull so as to find and remove the tumour had been a success, and that time would be the healer. Katse would be transported back to the house of Raggynil and hopefully, fully recovered in a matter of weeks and ready to succumb to a few tests to confirm the results. Pidlarch held the hand of the sleeping Katse and talked to her for a while, even though she was asleep. Pidlarch returned to the studio after spending many hours at the bedside of Katse, but she was still asleep when he left.

That was the last time Pidlarch (Jonathan) ever saw Paris, Katse and the rest of the café goers; he fell asleep in the studio on the *chaise longue*, with dreams of times just gone and times to come but woke up in the 'shopping trolley'. Jonathan looked around, and the coast was clear; out he jumped and ran home as quick as he could to avoid the bullies.

Not knowing if he would ever return to the places he 'dreams' of; not knowing if they, the memories, were true or the people were real. Wherever he was, whenever it was, who could say, but what he had learnt was the meaning of three things that, if practiced, were all that is needed for people to live alongside each other in harmony and peace; they are 'Love, Gratitude and Compassion'. As Katse, the love of his life is no longer in his grasp but is another memory, Jonathan struggles at times to come to terms with 'his gift' and can only hope that one day a return to those times in Paris, and the reality of the moon dancing upon the Seine is once more.

The moon shines upon the Seine.

Chapter 4
The Power of the Stones

Players: Chantitera, Chilti, Tandoness, Tablas, Tomiledo, Fraspled, Nariteg, Singeo, Phetomamric, Tiquatrez, Lottesuria.

This will be a story of the Stone-Age, of druids and worship, of contest, feasts, great henges, ditches, dykes and cursus avenues.

It is a summer's day which sees Jonathan and a friend fishing in the local river; they are knee deep on a section of rapids and wearing waders. They already have in their creels four brown trout of around 400g each and just enough to make an evening meal for their relative families. Jonathan made another cast with the excellent cane fly-rod with a greenheart top given to him by his grandfather, and this was his most treasured possession. This light, flexible rod flicked out one of Jonathan's home-made flies; this one he called a 'stripy dawn', made with pheasant feathers and small strands of black sheep wool. On this particular day, the fish were biting well but not always trout as there were shoals of dace vying for the few insects flitting across the calmer water of the eddies. Jonathan hooked into another trout, about the same size as the others so nothing special, but this would be enough for the meal. The fight lasted for a few minutes, and Jonathan was just about to slip his collapsible landing met under the fish when, lo and behold, two of the bullies appeared from the undergrowth and demanded the fish. These two bullies lived about two streets away from the home of Jonathan and not very friendly, but the advantage of wearing waders and standing thigh high in flowing water was enough to deter any contact, but the threat of throwing their rods in water as soon as they reach the bank was not to be ignored. The bullies waited until they came to firm ground, so there was little choice as they threw the five fish ashore, and in so doing, kept their rods at least.

They left with their ill-gotten gains, laughing at their good fortune, and Jonathan and his friend had little time left to catch the dinner. Jonathan did catch three more trout before leaving, and his friend another one, so that was two each which is a lot better than nothing. There was about a mile walk back to the arches of the bridge where the bikes were hidden, but on arriving, the bikes had gone, and in their place were, laying on the ground, two fish heads; it does not take much guessing where the bikes are now. Not only that, the thought of what Jonathan's father would say and do is best forgotten, but the leather belt would be felt for many days. Although this should not happen, it does, and it is the way of it, and one must bear the pain, for one day Jonathan will be able to leave his family home, the town in which he was born, the bullies and all. It was the next day on the way home from school that Jonathan was caught by the bullies who held him and tried to force him to eat a fish head. Jonathan offered to eat it if he could hold the fish, and they let go of his hands and gave him the fish head. There were four of them but suddenly, just as he lifted the head towards his mouth, Jonathan stepped slowly backwards, suddenly turned and fled, running like the wind; there was no catching him now as he headed for the wooded area and the refuge of the shopping trolley. Jonathan knew that he was safe for now, but the bullies would not be too happy the next time they met. Jonathan curls up, and again there are tears forming and slowly gliding down his cheeks as Jonathan gently descends into a peaceful rest.

Coming too, Jonathan is holding a pick crafted from the discarded antlers of a native red deer; his name is now Phetomamric, and all around him are others digging the earth each with antler picks. The air is clear, the warmth of a late spring day is felt upon his back as he fills another animal skin bucket with the soil and stone dug from what appears to be a huge trench. The bucket is collected by a broad-shouldered tower of a man called Tablas who greeted Phetomamric with the widest of smiles, showing gaps where teeth had been lost.

Five brown trout ready for the creel.

It was not long to the setting of the evening sun, and other workers were beginning to gather their tools and buckets, and after placing those in a small compound constructed from interwoven wicker branches, headed to the three wooden oblong thatched buildings. Looking back, Phetomamric could see a large mound around which was a partly dug ditch, the very same that, a few moments ago, he had been working in. This was to be the last resting place of 'Tandoness', the youngest son of the local chieftain, and with the internal stone-lined chamber already finished, there was just the ditch to complete and the soil distributed over the mound which, for the forty or so workers, would take no more than a couple of days. Tablas came from the northern isles of Orkney; his ancestors settled there and around the upper reaches of Scotland and beyond many generations ago after leaving the region of Norway in many ships (to note, this period is over 3000 years before the Vikings of the 8-9th centuries AD). Some of the settlements failed but most succeeded, and Orkney became the main base of these seafaring peoples creating a culture centred upon the use of stone. This culture encompassed construction of stone buildings and the erection of great monuments using giant slabs of local rock for that purpose. Now, Tablas and his team were moving southwards, not permanently, constructing earthworks and burial chambers for whoever required their expertise; this was the new trend radiating outwards from Orkney. The payment for this service was made with cattle and other domesticated animals, polished axes and gold; all of which could be used as barter for much-needed grain and other commodities, which would then be transported back by boat to the northern isles. Accompanying Tablas is his wife Lottesuria (the one with the red flowing locks which look like fire in the sun); they have been married for two years now and longed for a child of their own. Phetomamric belongs to the local tribe for whom Tablas is building the mound before the northern people move on to the next tribe who require the skills of Tablas and co. to build mounds and other monuments. For now, there is the refreshment of the fresh spring water, as cold as the winter snow and as crisp as a winter's dawn. Hands sore from the toils of digging were rubbed with the oils of a plant known as *altho* to the villagers, a word spoken by ancient travellers from the Greek islands (modern day Mallow). This would soften the hands and help with the healing; it was noted that none of the northern people required this treatment as almost all of them had hands as hard as mature leather. Fires kept the people warm as they talked about the mound and the hard work involved in its creation, but all were agreed that this new method of honouring the important dead would provide a living memory and perhaps, a focal point signifying a cultural expression of respect. Tablas was looking forward to the more challenging project of building a very large cursus which was a straight line of two banks set many yards apart, and anything from a few hundred yards to many miles in length and a possible henge (a circular monument) usually at least a hundred yards in diameter. These would be only the second to have been constructed in this country, but the order books are getting full for others. There was little for Phetomamric to do in the village, and it was with a sense of adventure that he had asked Tablas if an extra hand would be useful in building of the cursus and the favourable reply indicated that no help would be refused; especially from such a hard worker. It was with more than a little joy and expectation that Phetomamric lay to rest that night and at least, it would allow a couple of weeks for him to harden the hands in readiness for this venture. The next morning saw all the workers up early, eager to finish the circular ditch, for they all knew that a great feast would follow completion; as was the practice with all the great undertakings. Tablas gathered his professional builders and followed by the villagers march with good spirits towards the mound. Phetomamric, along with his close friends Chilti and Fraspled, gathered three antler picked each and joined the rest of the villagers on the short walk to the mound. Along the narrow path, it was more of a procession than a gathering with children lining the way shouting words of encouragement, wishing that they themselves could dig, but this was work for adults and hard work at that. There must had been over two hundred people there that day (another sixty of Tablas's people had arrive from another project), picks a swinging, soil a gathering and buckets emptying on the mounds. In some areas of the ditch, solid rock had to be cut though, and large hammer-stones were used to batter the rocks into manageable pieces and lifted by using the antlers as levers. Working as a small gang, there was more than a little rivalry amongst Phetomamric and his two friends, which, in fact, helped to achieve a good day's work; what you would call 'healthy rivalry' and in reality, more of a bonding exercise than anything else. With an excellent turnout during the day, the ditch was completed, and the village wise-man or druid known as Tiquatrez made an appearance, as was customary an offering, and a few wise words were forthcoming. A dozen or so antler picked, and a selection of polished stones were laid in the bottom of the last section of the ditch as a 'ritual deposit' to appease any earth spirits disturbed during the digging. With a light covering of soil, the items were buried for posterity.

Now, a great feast would ensue, both to celebrate the completion of the monument and to respect the person buried beneath the mound. From this feast, there would be other offerings consisting of some of the best joints of meat complete with bones, just to keep the spirits happy. Tablas's plans were to lead his workforce, by now, well over a hundred, away from the village, early the next morning, as it would take about two days to walk to the next project. Phetomamric acquired a large roasted leg of meat, located his friends Chilti and Fraspled and along with a wooden bowl of herbs filled their stomachs to fullness. They discussed the forthcoming project, and far from being apprehensive, all three were up for it and looking forward to the adventure. Just before they retired for the night, the druid Tiquatrez approached, as he had heard that they were leaving the village to assist with the cursus construction; he wished them well and gave them each a small quartz bead to hang around their necks. These beads would act as both, protection and as a reminder of the village and people that they are leaving behind, and the three accepted the amulets with honour; these beads would be handed back to the druid on their return. By the warmth of fire, they slept and in readiness had prepared all the clothes and equipment required for their journey.

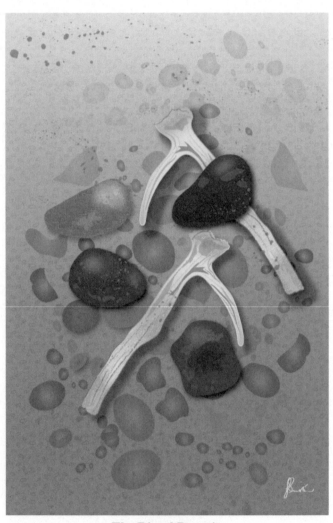

The Ritual Deposit.

The morning mists had not yet cleared when Phetomamric awoke, but Tablas was already mustering his people for an early start, so with some urgency Phetomamric shook his two friends, and they were soon up and tucked in breakfast, whatever was left on the now cold leg of meat. With a few goodbyes, off they went setting their sights to the south along the salt way through woods and across streams; the first day went well covering about 16 miles. The following day, the group arrive late in the day, greeted by another community; with just enough time for an initial inspection of the land across which the cursus was to be built. Tablas returned with the small group of overseers, and they spent the rest of the day discussing the project well into the night. Phetomamric and his three friends crashed out before finding out what part they would play in the in the construction process. As the sun rose, food was served and a call to assemble could be heard as Tablas gathered the workforce of near two hundred which was divided into five separate teams, with some to clear trees and shrubs, some to dig, some to carry, some to care (supply tools, food and water) and a small party of measurers. One of Tablas's overseers was Aillig whose job was to set out the extent of any construction including the direction and length. Now, Aillig was one short in his team as someone had broken his ankle on the walk from the last settlement, and it was Phetomamric who was allocated as a replacement. Aillig explained to him that the two would have with them two large carts full of ash poles, already collected yesterday; all a tall person high and sharpened at one end. The first four poles had been set into the ground last evening, perfectly aligned to the central star of Orion's belt as it reached its highest point in the sky during that year. That would be the direction of this three mile cursus, and cheekily Phetomamric asked if his two friends could drive the carts as they work well together as a team, and Aillig thought for a while before agreeing. That was a great sight to witness as they set out with the carts pulled by the oxen in readiness to set out the new processional route. Aillig and Phetomamric followed behind the carts, talking as they went, and one of the subjects that Aillig brought up was the fact that Tablas and Lottesuria had always longed for a child, but alas, they are without. Phetomamric had a little knowledge of the herbs and natural medicine available and remembered someone else in the village having the same problem which the druid had dealt with and resulted in a satisfactory outcome, but Phetomamric decides to say nothing until he had talked to the druid Tiquatrez. The line of stakes were soon to be seen stretching to the horizon, all perfectly in line, and already large groups of workers had completed a hundred yards of ditch and bank. All during the day, Phetomamric thought of the dreams and hopes of Tablas and Lottesuria and devised a plan to return, after the day's work, to the village and speak to Tiquatrez.

Phetomamric set off after the evening meal, as swift as the wind; with the way lit by the stars and the full moon, it took him over three hours to run back to his home village. Tiquatrez was found next to a small camp fire, contemplating the stars trying to make sense of the purpose of life and all. Phetomamric, catching his breath, presented the dilemma to the druid and asked about the portable grinders; grinders that he had seen being used many times. The druid explained that these little devices were only used by the British tribes to grind the fruit of the mistletoe but only the kind found in this country as other countries' mistletoe may be more harmful than good. The shape of the grinder matched the leaves of this mysterious plant which grew as a parasite on the branches of trees, especially the oak. The druid explained that the juices and seeds had been used for many years as a cure and number of medicinal purposes including fertility enhancement, and that he personally will collect and supply enough raw mistletoe and carve a couple of fresh grinders. These grinders which had been, in modern times, found in their hundreds, were apparently, in later ages, made from a variety of metals and showed various decorative finishes but all retained the basic curled leaf shape of the mistletoe.

Tiquatrez entered his round house and after a few minutes, came out with a good bunch of mistletoe which he had collected from the branches of an Oak tree on the sixth night of the moon after the winter solstice. A small incantation was offered to the goddess Frigga, and the names of Tablas and Lottesuria spoken aloud three times by the druid as he faced the moon. The items were then handed over to Phetomamric who carefully wrapped them in cloth and tied the ends with strips of willow bark before his journey back to the workers' camp; a journey which took until dawn to complete. There was no time for rest as the workers were already heading out to the cursus; missing one night's sleep was no hardship, as the sacrifice was for a worthy cause, and if good came of it, all the better. It was not until the end of the working day that Phetomamric caught up with Tablas and took the opportunity to explain the medicinal items wrapped inside the cloth.

It was thought best that both Tablas and Lottesuria swallowed a portion of the ground up mistletoe berries; a task that should be followed every day from one full moon to the next full moon.

Over the next couple of weeks, the cursus appeared as a long avenue surrounded by two edging banks, and the stone circle monument was measured out with a diameter of 40 yards, smaller than originally thought. The large stones for the circle required the whole workforce to drag them from the quarry over three miles away. This was done by using brute strength and many ash logs as rollers, bark intact, laid as a pathway along which the great stones could be dragged; there were seventy-two in all, and every one weighed in at over two tonnes. Indeed, the largest weighing in at a monstrous twenty tonnes took over forty people to drag across the landscape. This included the three pals Phetomamric, Chilti and Fraspled who heaved away guided by the rhythmical booming beat of a log drum; it actually took four days to accomplish that task. The tumultuous cheer could be heard many hills away as the great stone was finally slid by the way of a slope already dug just above the hole, setting it into its permanent position. Just to have been a small part of that feat would live long in the memories of all there, and no doubt tales of the achievement would embellish many fireside stories and legends for years to come. Apparently, most of these large stones were from outcrops of a type called oolitic limestone, in which could be found small crystals; these were the healing stones. Just like a modern battery, the sun's radiated energy was collected by these stones and was found to be beneficial to both the spirit and the body; that could be why we see people actually hugging the stones, subconsciously enjoying the healing power of the sun's radiation, mmm radio-therapy no less.

Magical mistletoe and grinder.

There was hope that both the cursus and the stone circle were finished for one of the main festivals called Lughnasadh; this marked the time of the great gathering, a time of celebrations, a time when hundreds of people would arrive from all the neighbouring tribes. The remaining stones should be in place on time, and the notcher Nariteg, whose job was to every day put a notch into the counting staff. A notch for every day of the year, there were now 212 cuts on the staff, and the festival was due to commence when the count was 232. This particular celebration was an even more special occasion as the head Druid had informed everyone that the dark spots that appeared on the surface of the sun would be at their maximum that year. The stones used to construct this circle which contained these small crystals or ooids naturally reacted with emissions caused by the sun spots, and this, in turn, gave certain power to the stone. This year would be the year that gave the stones maximum power and ability to heal, not only body but also mind. This phenomenon would not happen again for another eleven years; although, the stones would still be used, they would be less powerful. The power of the stones, during this period, has to be felt to be believed, and there would be no shortage of visitors participating during an extended period during the next month or so. The evenings were spent telling sagas and tales of great deeds of both mythical creatures and ancestral warriors.

There had not been a violent confrontation for many years, but this was now a period of peace and a time culture of farming, a time when communities had an opportunity to flourish and learn. On one of these long-enjoyable endings of the day, Tablas found the three friends congregated around a small campfire, just as Fraspled was in full flow, telling the story of a sea serpent called Jormungand. Tablas was quite amused at this because the tale must have come from one of his tribe; as it was a story originating from the northern islands, and Fraspled must have heard this tale from one of the workers who belonged to the mound builders and had remembered it well. Tablas sat down next to Phetomamric, greetings were exchanged, and all were in good spirits. Tablas turned his head towards Phetomamric, looked him straight in the eye with a great smile upon his face and patted him on the shoulder.

A Stone-hugger grabs tight.

There was exciting news concerning Lottesuria, news that brought cheer to all, news that the wife of Tablas was with child, and he thanked Phetomamric for providing the mistletoe and made a request to let Tiquatrez know of this news.

It was good that this ancient remedy had been a success, and that the wooden grinders were possibly the precursors to the metal grinders that have been widely found, during excavations and metal detecting surveys of Late Iron Age and early Roman contexts. In modern times, they have been called 'woad grinders' and 'cosmetic grinders', but now we know better because of their shape and the obvious similarity to the leaf of the mistletoe. No doubt, this statement will cause many discussions amongst historians who support the cosmetic and woad dye suppositions; but we know better, don't we?!

Not too many days had passed, and the whole thing was finished; the avenue forming the cursus looked magnificent and aligned perfectly to the highest point on the night sky that the central star of Orion's Belt, called Alnilam, reached its zenith. The great circle of stones appear ghostlike out of the morning mist; a wonderful and mysterious sight as the workers approached and began to remove all the excess soil and stone from the monuments. There were more and more people coming to the area; they numbered to hundreds, in readiness for the gathering and with them came a considerable number of domesticated animals including: sheep, cattle, goats and young pigs. The festival of *Lughnasadh* served dual purpose; firstly, to celebrate a good bounty from the fields, and secondly, to bond the relationships between neighbouring peoples. Both these things were as important as the other, and these celebrations took place but once a year, so every effort was made to make it a festival that would live on, not only, in the memories of all who took part but as tales and legends for years to come. Phetomamric and friends made every effort to integrate into the community, and so it passed that they became good friends of not only the workers of Tablas and the local tribe of which Tomiledo was chief but also many of the visiting peoples. The process of integration, of course, had to be practiced by the community as a whole, or else, it just *wasn't gonna* work, no matter how much of an individual effort was involved.

Everyone was looking forward to the great festival, a time when they would meet friends, relatives and strangers alike. One of the main parts of the celebrations would be the contests, for which there had been many months of training, and although the participants were friendly, they would be very competitive (this added to the excitement and therefore, made good entertainment). The contests consisted of athletic prowess in a number of disciplines such as: wrestling, spear throwing, feats of strength, dancing, running (an inbred love of fell racing and climbing hills and mountains, as if a hidden knowledge of such drives us on to the summit, and for what reason, who knows). Feasting brought happiness and the varied foodstuffs that were brought to the celebrations by hundreds of people would be consumed over a number of days and then the monuments would probably only be used again for these great gatherings. Matchmaking, the bonding of different people by selecting partners was all part of the festival, and all participants of a certain age would meet, converse and share a meal, a bit like a modern day speed-dating evening but more like an engagement commitment because whoever was mutually chosen, they entered a courtship resulting in an attachment (marriage) at the next festival in three months' time. There would be the traditional trading of gifts between the chief or spokesperson of each group, and these gifts were usually small but meaningful and symbolic; beautifully-polished stone axes, beads, rare shells and gold. The chief on whose land the celebrations took place also erected a stone carved with three identical (conjoined) faces looking in different directions; many hundreds of years later, this design manifests itself as the Roman god Janus, pronounced *Lanus* in Latin. (This type of effigy showing conjoined heads can be found in many countries in the form of a Brahma statue, a Buddha statue, a Lord Shiva statue, a Ganesh statue, Trimukha Gana Pathi and statues at Angkor Wat.) Tablas is taking the whole thing quite seriously and could be seen training at least twice a day, if not more; lifting heavier and heavier stones in readiness for one of the contests. Jonathan recalls that Phetomamric was concentrating on the running competition for which the runners would, with all cheering, attempt to recover one of three polished axes (hewn from an unusual green stone brought from the North West) placed upon the highest hill that could be seen from the stone circle at the end of the cursus. All of the events would bring prestige to the clan, tribe or group to whom the victor belonged; the games were the birthplace of legends, heroes and myths. Aillig would be dancing with Singeo, the first daughter of the local chief Tomiledo, and they too had been noticed practicing as they mimicked the flight of the insects; the fluttering of the butterfly, the hovering of the dragonfly and the dancing of the bee, and with what Phetomamric has witnessed, the pair were worth watching.

The first day of the festival had arrived, and everyone is busy preparing the fires, food, festivities, and flanks of the finest meats and practiced, out loud, their poetry and fables. There was noticeably more colour to be seen in the clothing, and checked patterns seemed to be 'in' that year. All the way along the avenue, there were: traders selling everything imaginable, dancers leaping gracefully, cooks basting beasts of many sorts, drummers a-banging and flutes a-trilling. There 'to be had' were wines, meads, beers, herbal concoctions and even fresh cool spring water. As the multitudes congregated along the route, the elders, great warriors and tribal chief *et al* gathered at the beginning of the avenue and waited for the chief druid, who was none other than Tiquatrez himself. Looking back, there could be seen, dressed in robes and walking with magnificently-carved sticks, a small group of druids. A great sight as they took their rightful place at the front and began a slow walk along the avenue towards the stone circle. The throngs of people part, without hesitation and utter salutations, cheered and waved their arms in recognition of their leaders and carried on with the celebrations as soon as the procession had passed. When the circle of stones reached the elite form, a large circle and the local chief Tomiledo was the first to sit; others, according to their importance (rank), began to sit either side of the local chief until the circle was complete. The druids performed the required ritual, blessing the earth and all that walked and crawled upon it and then sat in the centre of the circle. The best cuts of meat were carried to the circle along with large leather wine bags, and they eat, drank and talked a plenty.

Now, it was the turn of the athletes, dancers and poets to perform at their best beginning with the poetry contest, and it was the sister of Lottesuria, named Chantitera, who was first to approach the circle of stones and recite her practiced lines. In keeping with the celebrations, Chantitera had purposely chosen as her subject something close to everyone's heart, a light-hearted look at the most popular drink of the day. There hung over the gathered multitude an air of silence and anticipation as everyone turned towards the orator (Jonathan only remembers the first two stanzas as best he could; which I duly record below).

An Ode to Barley

My head, it pounds, to sounds, and light o' glee
Mine blessing of good cheer, came yesterday
The eyes are blurred, but still I may see
Is so cursed as the price I did pay
So sweet, in tasting, so smooth it downed
More begged more, as smiles increase, with time
Once the ground be broken, sweat as toiled
Planted, said seed, at measured pace, by hand
So small, yet harmless, it may, look to me
Fine spirits concocted, once boiled

With methodic movement, of wooden hoe
This mystery, ensues beneath, when is sown
No thought of liquid, or any, future woe
The power, of the brew, be wary, be known
Nurtured, watered, tended, and more
Cultivated, reaped, dried and fed
Green leafed, sprout like arms, aloft, do stretch
Blue skies, red skies, black skies, cloudy and all
Hale, to barley, hark, to soil manured
Give caring, to remove, encroaching vetch.

There would have been a certain 'meter' or rhythmic beat to the reading of the ode with the accent on the second word or syllable, for which I have included an example of the possible tempo below:

Phonic Interpretation of An Ode to Barley

My **head**,| it **pounds**,| to **sounds**,| and **light**| o'glee
Mine **bless**|-ing **of**| good **cheer**,| came yes|-ter-**day**
The **eyes**| are blurr|-**ed**, |but **sti**|-ll **I**| may **see**
Is **so**| curs-**ed**| as **the**| price **I**| did **pay**
So **sweet**,| in **tast**|-ing, **so**| smooth **it**| down-**ed**
More **begg**|-ed **more**,| as **smiles**| in-**crease**,| with **time**
Once **the**| ground **be**| brok-**en**,| sweat **as**| toil-**ed**
Plant-**ed**,| said **seed**,| at **meas**|-ured **pace**,| by **hand**
So **small**,| yet **harm**|-less, **it**| may, **look**| to **me**
Fine **spir**|-its, **are** |con-**coct**|-ted, **once**| boil-**ed**.

With **meth**|-od-**ic**| move-**ment**,| of **wood**|-en **hoe**
This **myst**|-ery, **en**|-sues **be**|-neath, **when**| is **sown**
No **thought**| of li|-quid, **or**| any, **fu**|-ture **woe**
The **pow**|-er, **of**| the **brew**,| be **wary**,| be **known**
Nur-**tur**|-ed, **wat**|-er-**ed**,| tend-**ed**,| and **more**
Cul-**ti**|-va-**ted**,| reap-**ed**,| dri-**ed**| and **fed**
Green **leaf**|-ed, **sprout**| like **arms**,| al-**oft**,| do **stretch**
Blue **skies**,| red **skies**,| black **skies**,| clou-**dy**| and **all**
Hale, **to**| bar-**ley**,| hark, **to**| soil **man**|-ur-**ed**
Give **car**|-ing, **to**| re-**move**,| en-**croach**|-ing **vetch**.

Many more were read that day by a number of bards and poets, and now the circle of elders casted their votes; each had six small pebbles which were to be casted into cupped-shaped hollows on the ground (a hollow for each poem or ode); three pebbles to their choice of best, two to their choice of second, and one to their choice of third. The pebbles were counted, and the winner with 94 pebbles announced as being an elder from one of the surrounding tribes, and second prize of a beautifully-fashioned stone axe went to Chantitera who earned 67 pebbles. This achievement gave a little lift to, not only, Tablas and Lottesuria but also to Phetomamric who was about to take his place for the mountain running event. There were over forty runners for this event which covered 15 miles of rough terrain up to the highest point on one of the nearby hills, across the river through the wooded slopes and up to the summit. Off they went, accompanied by lots of cheers and a whole load of arm waving. Phetomamric was quick away and, actually, led as they swam the river. Up the hill to the wood and still leading, but two runners flew by, and it was now a race for survival on the approach to summit. Phetomamric was more than happy to pick up one of the polished stone axes in the third place. Now, for the return to the finish at the stone circle but running down hill was far more dangerous than running up, and it wasn't too long before runners were stumbling and falling over the many roots and stones. Unfortunately, Phetomamric was amongst the fallers, but he has more resolve and shook himself down, picked himself up and carried swiftly on. With a couple of cuts and a few bruises for his efforts, he reached the finish-line in a good third place and was more than pleased with that effort. Now, it is the turn of Tablas, who was up against some giants of men, and the task set before them appeared, to the lesser-muscled onlookers, almost impossible. The task was to lift and carry six great stones set ten yards apart along the avenue, dropping the first when they reach the second, then dropping the second when they reach the third, and so on. There were preliminary rounds until only the five strongest remained, and Tablas was one of these. It looked like the whole gathering had now lined the avenue in anticipation of the final of the contest. The chief Tomiledo stood proud holding his favourite shield which he would raise above his head and bring down as a signal to start. All five were limbering up by touching their toes, stretching their backs and extending their ample arms; Jonathan tells me that Tablas felt good to go and even showed a broad smile as he greeted the other four finalists. The shield was raised; the competitors were ready and looking at Tomiledo, down the shield went, and the first stones were lifted and off they went. No one dropped the first stone, which was oblong in shape, until the second was reached; this stone looked a little awkward, a little heavier as well as being shaped like a kidney. All five made it to the third stone, and there was no more than three yards from first to last as they struggled to get the perfectly square (actually a cube), and again heavier than the previous two, actually off the ground. All accomplished the lifting, but two dropped the stone halfway to the next, but one managed to lift up the stone and carry on. Tablas was still in contention at this stage. Only four competitors reached stone number four which was shaped like a pillar and really heavy but, all four remaining lifted this monster and taking very small steps proceeded along the avenue accompanied by shouts, cheers and hand clapping. It was with delight that all four made it to the fifth stone which was rough and really no shape at all, just a huge unfinished boulder, and a sight to see, all of them were in a line as they eyed up the last; a truly magnificent ball of stone. There was no set time limit, and all that was required was to be the first person just to reach the ring of stones, where all the elders and dignitaries sat. Of the four, only three managed to even lift the ball. Tablas managed about six yards but could go no further and could only watch as the two remaining (now sweating, red-faced and panting) challengers painstakingly waddling duck-like slowly forward. The victor crossed the entrance into the circle of stones when both the winner and the great stone ball dropped to the ground. Tablas and the rest of the strong participants congratulated the winner who was, by now, sitting up and breathing deeply to replenish all the oxygen levels. Tablas was most pleased because he had done the best he could, and that is all that could be expected from a person. Because of the tremendous physical efforts that these strongest members of their respective communities displayed, chief Tomiledo gave five gold torques to the druid Tiquatrez to present to each finalist in the stones challenge (the chief apparently enjoyed watching feats of strength and was probably a little over generous as regards to prizes).

The festival was going well, and everyone was having a great time, whether they were making new friends, catching up with old friends or just enjoying the feasting; these were 'good times'. Phetomamric and friends congratulated Tablas on his efforts and admired the gold torque which according to Tablas would be taken back to the Islands and used as currency for the benefit of his tribe. In the meantime, the torque would be buried and collected on the way back (along with others accepted as payment for all the construction work) after the next project, which was in the west. Tablas let it be known that Phetomamric and friends were welcomed to tackle the next adventure, if they so wished. Tomorrow was matching day when partners would be mutually accepted, and bonds made between the different tribes and peoples; bonds that would cement friendship and understanding. It had been a long tiring day, but a good day, and now, Phetomamric was looking forward to some well-earnt sleep as well as looking forward to tomorrow.

Jonathan opens his eyes and sees the side of the shopping trolley, and there is a realisation that another adventure in another time has come to an end. There is an eerie quietness, no voices could be heard, and the coast is clear as Jonathan disembarks from the safety of his steel sanctuary. Jonathan makes a swift departure and runs as fast as wind towards home. What he has learnt from this latest escapade are a number of things: winning is good for the soul but not essential, for as long as you give your utmost best at whatever you do; it is all that is required, and one must congratulate the victors and admire their skills and expertise.

Follow your dreams, for they disappear if you don't grab the opportunity, come what may.

If you can help someone, just do it without expecting any reward; that's not a bad philosophy at all and should be taken as part of your reason for life.

Take every opportunity to learn something new; whether it be a new skill or a new alternative way of thinking.

Jonathan becomes rather quiet and a little inward as he tries to explain the realisation that these experiences are real, well real to him at least. The fact that he may never know how things turn out, as it is beyond his comprehension, and that he may never meet these people again, and if he does, will he arrive where he left off or would he be ten years younger or forty years older? Thoughts of dreams, or are they dreams of thought? The next adventure, if you could call it that, is dark in content, frightening in part and probably a time and place Jonathan does not wish to see again; it is a tale of fortitude, fear, faith and favour.

Chapter 5
The Mystery of the Winged Helmet

Players: Beckaria, Shanakew, Nella, Holmenca, Lishlag, Anvo, Neeba, Yeniblod, Deladuc, Dosiwec.

For pocket money Jonathan had a number of avenues to earn welcoming cash, such as: catching fish (brown trout and sea trout caught with the 'dry fly' or tickled from the streams) and sold to the local fishmonger or picking blackberries and mushrooms which were then taken fresh to the local market greengrocers. Every morning Jonathan would be up with the lark to deliver papers, this involved sorting the papers into two rounds which, unfortunately, covered both sides of the town, and when the trusty bicycle succumbed to a puncture, the task of delivering involved running on foot the whole way carrying a full delivery bag. The paper round worked wonders for Jonathan's ability to sustain a good turn of foot which in turn found him enlisted into the school cross-country team.

One particular Sunday morning out delivering papers, which, unfortunately, involved passing one of the houses in which the eldest of the bullies lived, Jonathan was confronted and stopped by two bullies who grabbed his bike. It was fortunate that Jonathan could jump off and run followed closely by his antagonists. Heading for the woods, Jonathan soon left them behind; now, one of the benefits of cycling regularly was his ability to sustain a good head of steam. The wood reached. Jonathan found the shelter of the trolley, climbed in, curled up and rued his lot; at least he was safe and let the mind, or should I say, soul, take over.

Jonathan slips quietly into another land, another life and hears, or so he recalled to me, strange music, a mix of drums, flutes, chanting and shrieks. He (Jonathan) was now named Lishlag, a young boy, somewhere warm and most likely in the

Near East; as far as we could work out a land known to the ancients as Mesopotamia (what a great sounding name). The air was filled with aromas from fresh spices and roasting lamb or goat, but the most homely of smells emanated from piles of freshly cooked bread. This was one of the supply depots used to replenish the food baskets of the many warriors belonging to the army of Alexander the Great, encamped just below the hills and mountains of Taurus. His best friends Holmenca, the fourth son of a camel trader (forerunner of the camel army of the desert regions), Yeniblod the only son of the widow Shanakew (wife of the mighty Dosiwec) and Beckaria (although an orphan, she was cared for by the family of Lishlag). Beckaria was a descendent of a once great warrior called Deladuc, the very same who had captured, with the help of Dosiwec, a silver helmet from one of Shalmanesar III generals. Deladuc added the golden wings to this magnificent polished silver headdress which could now be found in the forbidden part of the camel and goatskin tent; which was the home of Lishlag's extended family. The golden wings were fashioned on the wings of the Lammergeier, a giant of a bird, a bird of prey often seen soaring amongst the rare clouds ready to pounce with its huge talons and monstrous beak. Unlike other winged helmets which displayed wings that projected upwards, these golden wings sloped downwards as if the helmet was the incarnate body of this great bird which, when in flight, displayed a wingspan of nearly three yards. When no one was looking, Lishlag and his friends would try on this helmet, the weight of which kept them anchored to the spot, and it was no mean feat for two people to actually lift it at all. The helmet of Qarqar was its name, and the hero named Deladuc wore this helmet sporting wings of gold which flickered and shone during the battles giving the effect of appearing to be in more than one place at a time. This young group of friends grew up, washed in these legends as many a time they had hid near the camp fires and eavesdropped on the stories told by both the warriors and their descendants.

Many times, there can be read in the histories of conquering nations, stories of peoples led by powerful rulers, such as the Assyrian king Shalmanesar III, who had carved a great kingdom and saw many great battles. Lishlag grew up embroiled in these legends of battle and war which saw many lands laid waste during the creation of vast empires. It was now the turn of the

Persians and the armies of Darius to sweep across the lands establishing the next great empire. It was a desperate time in which many survival skills were learnt at an early age, and it was the younger generation who had seen their brothers, fathers and grandfathers become legends and the subjects of folk tales; tales that were told over the twinkling embers of countless campfires. Now is the turn of the young leaving families behind, not with sadness but with pride, honour, strength and hope to join the armies of Alexander of Macedon, also called 'Alexander The Great' against a formidable adversary, the Persians. Many a people had trembled at the mere utterance of the name of Persia and the powerful ruler Darius with an army so vast that the earth trembled when they marched. They, the young of Greece, were ready, and there was no fear, no sadness, but the tears of loved ones and the waving of banners, shouts of encouragement to these 'bands of brothers' who had known each other throughout childhood and beyond.

Lishlag and Holmenca, because of their expertise in the art of riding camels, had enlisted in the cavalry of Alexander, and two cousins Neeba and Anvo joined as part of a *dekas* (a ten man team forming part of a unit of phalanx, the long spear holders).

The Battle of Gaugamela, sometimes called either Arbela or Erbil, was fought on the first day of October in the year 331BC. The morning was cool with a slight wind making the air a little dusty to the eye; there was a lot of noise, the sharp hammering of the blacksmith, still turning out swords, spears and the odd helmet repairs; the food preparation seemed to always make singing and chanting compulsory amongst the bakers; the whinnying of horses, baa's of sheep and goat, even laughter could be heard. The camp was stirring like some great awakening. Ah, the aromas, now that was something that could not be forgotten; there was something magical in the memory of smells as Johnathan recalls one of his favourites, the unforgettable odours of decaying leaves disturbed during an autumnal search for conkers. A heaving mass of humanity individually setting to task, almost robotically, carrying out their orders, duties and personal tasks as if oblivious to the pending battle and the coming together of two great armies; to this band of heroes, it was just another day amongst days.

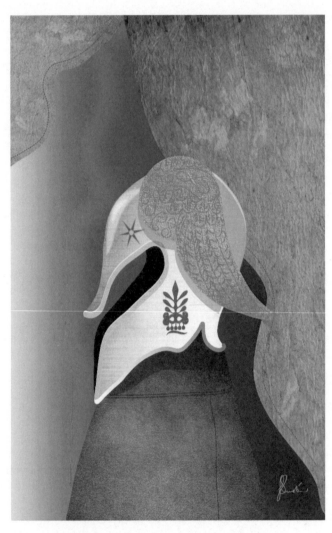

The helmet of Qarqar worn by Deladuc.

Lishlag polished the helmet tenderly, lovingly with soft wool of the sheep, the natural oil of lanolin cleaning, preserving and burnishing the silver and gold, oh, a sight to grasp as if it were a gift from the gods. It shone as if it emitted its own light; others crowded around to witness the wonder and many would tell the tale, a spectacle to behold. The armour cleaned, and weapons laid out, sharpened, waxed and offerings donated to all powers believed natural or spiritual; the time to partake in the battle meal was now. A hearty meal would make an army full at belly and satisfied in mind; this was a time to remember the heroes of the past and tales of not only daring do and glory but of cementing thoughts of loved ones, family and friends, as those people left behind would be thinking of these men, warriors and heroes. Lishlag joked, as he stroked the charm that hung about his neck, that he could hear the voice of his dear and beloved friend Beckaria, who had gifted the beautiful heart-shaped jewel of amber. Inside the amber could be seen a magnificent specimen of the *Lucanus cervus* (stag beetle) preserved for eternity within the golden mass of a

Baltic treasure gifted to Deladuc many years ago by ancient travellers from the north.

There could be seen a dust storm to the east accompanied by an ever-increasing indescribable noise, a sort of mixture of a rumbling thunder and a metallic echo as if it was the rattling of ten thousand bronze buckets being dragged by ten thousand snorting horses; above this, there is heard frightening melodic, high pitched, haunting, piercing, shrieking reverberations that could be loosely called music, sending spine chilling shivers through the mid-morning air.

The Persians were close, so vast that the greatest plague of locusts ever seen would fill, but one shoe of those who tread towards the camp; it seemed as if the whole land, woods, valleys, fields, rivers and mountains had turned into armies of demons and fiends. Here was the army of Darius, the great Persian, who had levelled the battlefield for his advantage, removing any barriers that would hinder such vast multitudes of horses, chariots and men.

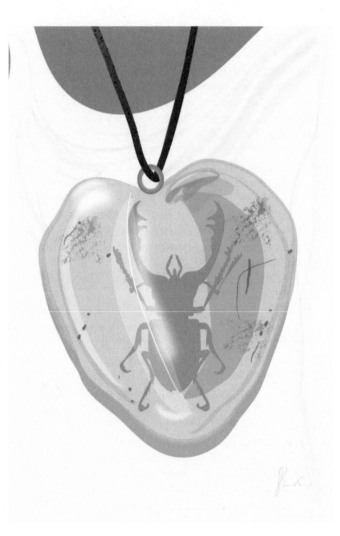

The magnificent amber charm with stag beetle.

This was not for the faint of heart, and the battle proper had yet to come, but where we feared in heart and mind, there is no place in our minds for such things; there were knowing glances and nodding of heads that this was the hour, this was the day when friends and allies fought as one for a common cause, freedom. Freedom of land, freedom of family, freedom to believe, freedom of people young, old and unborn, who in defeat, would make the journey to the land of ancestors carrying shield, spear and hope and a certain remembrance in the mouths and minds of generations to come. The morning meal finished, and goat-skin drinking vessels suckled upon to clear dry throats and added the much-needed liquid to extinguish the thirst in preparation and expectation of not knowing from where the next drop may come.

Horses saddled with soft-padded cloaks, looking magnificent in the morning sun, fed and watered, were gathered into their respective regiments in readiness for mounting. Lishlag and Holmenca presented themselves dressed in a tunic, with no armour because of refusal of Alexander to wear any protection; it was thought better to copy that example. Although, Lishlag did adorn his head with the infamous Winged Helmet, and Holmenca sported an undecorated bronze helmet. The weapons they carried consisted of a spear, which had a spearhead at both ends, along with a sword and surprisingly, no shield was carried by the cavalry.

There appeared to be a great horde far out-flanking the army of Alexander, and the instructions received by Lishlag and Holmenca were to extend the cavalry line to try and cover the overlapping Persian multitude. There was no time to be fearful; there was a job to do, and already the Persians were trying to take advantage of their numbers by menacingly encircling Alexander the Great's outnumbered army, so much so that the supply waggons were in danger of being destroyed. This was where the two friends Lishlag and Holmenca were leading a charge of five hundred cavalry; the noise was deafening, hoofs pounding the hard earth, and the battle cries resounding from the hills. The dust blew up, enshrouded the charge as if a great smoke-breathing monster had appeared from the ground itself. Above the dust, the only things visible were the tips of the spears and the glinting, gleaming golden wings of the 'winged helmet'; a sight to behold as this squadron of cavalry halted the Persians attempt to attack the rear. Alas, during the fierce fighting, Holmenca had sustained a leg injury from a Persian lance and had been brought down. Lishlag had heard his cry and circled back as soon as the opposing force was halted. Calling the name of his friend as the unit regrouped, but there was no reply to be heard, and Lishlag had sorrow in his eyes, but there was no time to dwell as the main battle was now at a crucial stage. With great losses on both sides the charge saved the flank of the Alexandrian infantry and allowed the Macedonian general to launch a headlong attack directly at Darius, the Persian King. Alexander, having seen a victory on the left flank, launched this great charge, and on seeing this, Lishlag followed with half the cavalry squadron, leaving the remainder to protect the left flank. The army caught sight of the winged helmet shining as if it was a beacon through the dust, and large numbers of infantry followed in hot pursuit; horses snorting, clashing of metal against metal, foe against foe. The rider who wore the winged helmet was at Alexander's side as the momentum of the charge cleared a path leading to Darius, who turned his chariot and fled from the battle; the battle was won, the Persian domination was all but over.

Alexander had again shown a mastery in the art or tactics, even against overwhelming odds; the celebrations were kept at a minimum due to the losses in the battle, but, nonetheless, there could be seen acknowledgement of the great deeds and heroic acts. It was now left to the followers to clear the fields of weapons, armour, horses and tend to the wounded. It was just in time when Beckaria, who had been helping with the baggage train as part of a group, was making thousands of loafs of bread to nourish the army of Alexander and helping with the wounded, one of whom was none other than Holmenca. Another coincidence as Yeniblod, who being a little younger and not yet trained in the art of warfare, was driving a cart loaded with some of the spoils of the battle, happened to pass by and was recognised by Beckaria. Between the two of them, Holmenca, who was barely conscious and bleeding from a gaping leg wound, was gently lifted and settled amongst a bed of spears to be transported back to the main camp but not before Beckaria had covered the injury with leaves of the plant yarrow (a recognised herb used to stem the flow of blood) commonly called 'wound healer' and sealed with fresh horse dung to keep any bacteria and dust out.

Back at the camp, Lishlag took stock of what remained of his cavalry unit, cleaned and fed the horses, and only then did they head for one of the many campfires and food. Beckaria, handing out the large flat loafs, was warmly greeted by Lishlag who was somewhat saddened by the loss of Holmenca, his dear friend, companion, brother in arms. Beckaria grabbed Lishlag, one hand on each shoulder and informed Lishlag that Holmenca is in one of the tents badly wounded but still alive. Lishlag thanked her and with no regard for food, ran to the tent which Beckaria had pointed out and found his dear friend; although, there had been other warriors who he had known to have perished on the field, Lishlag knew the importance of a life-long friend. Although, the yarrow poultice had staunched the bleeding wound on the leg of Holmenca, but because of the time laying on the battlefield it had succumbed to infection, and it was all too apparent that the leg had to be amputated for him to survive. There were others actually worse off, and Holmenca would have to wait in turn, and all Lishlag could do was to offer comfort. It was not until after the eating period had finished that Lishlag returned to the injury tent were Holmenca had again slipped into unconsciousness; this could be good as there would be no pain during the removal which would be from the upper thigh, it had to be. You could see where the infection was creeping upwards, but the time was now, and the person best prepared to perform this task was a local butcher who had many years of cutting and chopping experience of animal bones ready for consumption; that was the way of things, and no one was better suited. Although, there was, somewhere in the camp, a dedicated surgeon, but there was little time to waste. The small group of friends gathered around to offer both moral and spiritual support and watched, with compassion, as the knives and axes went swiftly to work. Not more than a few minutes had gone by when the infected limb was removed and the blood vessels sealed. Just in time, as the arrival of Nella, the surgeon, looking a little worn out and overworked, was met with more than a few sighs, and the remaining skin was neatly folded and stitched with strands of animal sinew, wrapped in antiseptic herbs; only rest and tender care would now act as a catalyst to recovery.

It was three days and nights before Holmenca opened his eyes and another two days before the journey home could commence, and this small band of friends set forth back to the village. There was an agreement between the travellers that the most important goal was to return together, taking turns to look after wounded Holmenca as best they could. The journey was made easier because of the two camels and six Persian horses rounded up after the battle; the strongest of which was used to drag the wooden stretcher, woven from strong but supple withies and lined with soft grasses, upon which Holmenca lay. The first night, camped, rested, nourished, with all in good spirits, songs were sung, tales were told and smiles could be seen in the reflection of the warm glow of the crackling embers. This was the first night for months that a restful sleep could be guaranteed, and this band of friends: Lishlag, Holmenca, Neeba, Anvo, Beckaria and Yeniblod lay beneath the stars in quiet contemplation. There were many shooting stars seen that clear but cool night, and coupled with a full moon, the signs were favourable, a good omen.

Jonathan sighs, an uneasy realisation in his eyes that he was recalling a life and not a dream, a happening, a truth; not to mention my own eagerness to listen and record these wonders which are now passed on by my pen to you, the reader, as if you are actually journeying through time, page by page, adventure by adventure (Jonathan with a slight tremble in his voice continued the tale).

This small caravan was now in sight of the village they had left many weeks ago, and there was a sense of expectation in the air as they trod on all too familiar land, lands of their forefathers, land that they had fought to preserve. Shanakew, who was washing clothes in a nearby stream, was the first to recognise who this band of travellers were, and there were shrieks of delight which brought the rest of the village to life. Unshackling the sledge, which had been the bed of the injured Holmenca, Yeniblod quickly told the story of the battle to the widow of Dosiwec and with the help of others carried the still unconscious Holmenca out of the heat of the sun into the tent of Shanakew. A vigil, shared by all, was kept over the weakening wounded warrior with water carefully fed drop by drop, dripping into his mouth and cool swabs smoothing sweat away from his brow.

Almost a week had passed when one morning, Jonathan could not recall who was on watch at the time, the eyes of Holmenca twitched and opened, and there was excitement beyond belief. All the care and sleepless nights had been worth the effort as most often what you contribute into life you get out, is returned in kind, and Holmenca had always put others first. The first task for Anvo was to fashion, out of the best hardwood, a splendid crutch to aid his dear friend to stand, walk and generally achieve some resemblance of a normal life. Everyone was so kind, and it was not long before Holmenca was seen around the village assisting where he could. So much care had gone into the recovery process that it came as no surprise that a love bond had formed between Beckaria and Holmenca, so much so that a wedding was planned, and the couple had asked Lishlag to give away the bride (as an elder would have done). A great feast was prepared, fires were lit and again the aromas of fresh bread, spices and fine roast filled the air. The stars sparkled in the deep azure skies, a calm and magical evening with the sound of crackling kindling as the food was cooked and the occasional laughter as tales were told by the tellers of truth and myth alike.

There was little thought of battle, fighting and pain; just happiness, love and smiles; war and conflict, at times, cannot be avoided but should not be sought after nor wished for, for war is an evil in itself but sometimes, an unavoidable necessity. The bride, who was dressed in finest silk with many coloured beads adorning the head and looking a picture of serenity, was walked around the village boundary. This was an ancient practice, showing not only her commitment to the bonding, but also a statement that she was willing to share the chores of the community. There came now the camels, decorated with all manner of brightly-coloured blankets and beads woven into hide hairs, mounted by musicians playing flutes and drums led by Neeba and Anvo. The widow Shanakew, with the help of fellow villagers, could be seen carrying very ornate stacks of pottery.

The inviting campfires and bread oven.

These were a collection that the mighty Dosiwec had brought back from one of the campaigns; these were from one of the Halaf sites of Mesopotamia consisting of highly decorated jars, goblets and bowls; all a gift to the new bride. The ceremony of partnership was held in the sanctity of the tent where the oaths, chants and dedications were exchanged, all under the watchful eyes of the village elders.

There were no rings exchanged between the couple, only gifts, and Beckaria drew back a goatskin that had been laying in the corner to reveal a magnificent saddle embellished by silver threads accompanied by a handwoven saddle blanket, a colourful piece of work which had taken Beckaria many months to make on a loom kept secret from all the friends. Even without the missing leg, Holmenca was still quite an accomplished horseman, and his eyes sparkled at the sight of these gifts. Lishlag in reply had gathered jewels from the northern tribes; there were rubies and rich blue Lapis lazuli (the same colour that can be seen as eyebrows on the funeral mask of Tutankhamun) set in gold and silver. Also, Lishlag, with the help of the local silversmith, had designed a truly wondrous necklace and earing set, which justly matched the beauty of Beckaria. Although these were valuable gifts in their own rite, it was the giving that mattered, and their worth was only measured against the love and sincerity of the offering.

A speech by Lishlag indicated, reading between the lines, that he (Lishlag) was more than fond of Beckaria, but perhaps it was what we would call 'brotherly love', such was the closeness of the friends we will never know. It was then that Lishlag went on to describe the love and dedication that bonds all friends and gives a moral 'that you must never forget your close friends' as they are part of you, they are you; without them you are not you; they are part of your soul and you are theirs; know the power of this and cherish these friends. Lishlag wished the couple a long life and imparted to Holmenca that when his friend was in need of a crutch, let him be at his side, and that he (Lishlag) would be that crutch, both mentally and physically forever, no questions asked. The winged helmet was the gift from Lishlag to the couple with the stipulation that it was cherished and passed down to their first born, and the stories of great deeds told in the light of their fires, with the hope that they, who wear it and tell the tales, do not need to use it in battle.

News of this union had travelled far and wide and caught the ears of one of the ancient tribes of the north, the king of which had a memory of the name 'Holmenca'. As many years ago, his son, who was called such, had been taken whilst playing in the fields, taken by camel traders never to be seen again. This king had made the journey out of curiosity and hope because the name Holmenca was unusual amongst the southern people. A great number of camels could be seen heading towards the village, the dust bellowing from the sides of the approaching host. The villagers looked at each other anxiously, believing it to be an approaching army and feared for their lives, but an out rider, on reaching the village, informed the elders that his master came bearing gifts for the couple who have pledged their love for each other. There must had been over two hundred camels and as many splendidly-armoured solders astride their mounts followed by a dozen camels each carrying parts a great tent ,and at the fore was an old-bearded man dressed in fine silks highlighted with golden threads. Upon the belt of the bearded one could see a fabulous dagger encrusted in jewels, and in his long white beard, there were many beads which shone and sparkled in the sunlight; this was a king if ever there was. The villagers had never before seen the like and cleared a space on the south side of the settlement, and everyone assisted in the construction of the biggest tent ever seen. On the floor of which were laid magnificent carpets of many colours and designs leading to an inner chamber adorned with the finest curtains and exquisitely-carved wooden seats; it was from here that the king asked that the couple be brought ,and the villagers to stand at the entrance to the inner chamber but not to enter.

The villagers gathered as requested, and the followers of the king tended to the campfires and preparation of food so none would be spoilt or burnt before the celebration feast commenced. Two of the king's biggest warriors guided Holmenca and Beckaria to the inner chamber, with the rest of the villagers jostling for the best view; the couple knelt before this king who instructed the couple to sit on the two carved chairs on each side of the king. The king then asked Holmenca to raise his right arm high into the air and there could be seen a bright red birthmark on the inside of the arm; it had the shape of a teardrop about the size of a thumbnail. The king removed his golden threaded silk cloak, and on lifting his right sleeve, held up his wrinkled weather-beaten arm to reveal the very same birthmark; there was an audible gasp from the villagers followed by the quietest silence that ever was heard. The king, aided by his two bodyguards, stood and proclaimed to the gathering that Holmenca, indeed, was his lost grandson. The only son of the king was killed in battle, and therefore, the king vowed that it would be his responsibility to look after Holmenca, now identified as the only son of his only son and the king's only grandchild. This grandchild and heir to the throne was the victim of kidnapping, and after the camel traders had stolen the young two-year-old child, the king, in his grief, fathered no more children. The king rejoiced and declared that Holmenca was the lost prince and heir to his kingdom, and that Beckaria has now the status of a Princess. That was not all because this village had cared for and saved the life of the prince, a gift of fertile lands to the north was offered in thanks. Holmenca (now a Prince) held the right arm of the king, and Beckaria (now a Princess) held the left arm as the three of them, followed by all the villagers, made their way to the feasting area.

The feast continued for many days. The campfires were bright, and many tales were told; a sight to behold was Holmenca wearing the winged helmet of Qarqar, and by his side could be seen the crutch crafted by Anvo, surrounded by the children of the village, telling a story of great deeds, mysteries and heroes. Looking on was the bearded figure of a great but very old king, on whose face could be seen the biggest smile ever seen, from ear to ear and even beyond; into the night. I could see a watering in the eyes of Jonathan as he explained that although this adventure had taken what seemed like years, not more than thirty minutes had passed in the sanctuary of the shopping trolley as he opens his eyes to find himself alone in the woods, as he peers from the safety of the trolley, and as far as he is concerned, this was not a fanciful dream but a reality remembered. I did ask Jonathan if he is going back to that land, that time, that love, the next time he seeks refuge in the shopping trolley, but surprisingly, to me, Jonathan had seemingly no control over where or even what time in history he may end up, and that he may never see these people again.

I had wondered if the actual trolley was some sort of time machine, but it was no more than a piece of metal, and that the amazing powers of transporting himself, his mind, his being, were Jonathan's alone. It was very brave of Jonathan to tell someone of these, supposedly, past lives, as these tales could have been met with ridicule and malice. So, as narrator and transcriber of the words of Jonathan, I do so without drawing upon personal conclusions as to the validity of even a single word. I, as the writer of these tales, offer them as words of truth until there is conclusive evidence presented before me to the contrary. I await the next time we speak when Jonathan would share his adventures with me. It is not for me to say if these tales are true or not, but in his eyes and from his mouth, there are other lives that maybe we all have lived, only to be remembered by few.

The birthmark is revealed.

Chapter 6
The Mallet, the Chisel and the Sky

Players: Grantiplis, Fymyla, Syfelldam, Goldyfran, Shappergors, Cetrick, Egwari, Bludigesh, Daphi, Trelbytuf, Bebelumbe, Cripnoos.

    The morning is warm, and Jonathan is thinking of a bike ride maybe over the moors where fossils could be found in an old quarry. Looking out of the window, Jonathan could see two groups of children facing each other, some holding sticks, and it looks like one end of the street against the other. Not a regular occurrence but always on the cards, and soon the parents were on the scene and sorted it all out. Jonathan could see among them, three of the regular bullies who were most likely the main instigators of the confrontation. So, although it now appeared safe for Jonathan to venture out, he was wary that there could be problems. Jonathan checked his bike just to make sure the tyres were pumped up and away he went. Heading for one of his friend's houses, he was soon being trailed by two riders; so, to save any confrontation, Jonathan took off like a rocket and was pretty confident that he could outrun the two bullies, but they did give chase, shouting and waving their arms. They were gaining ground on a flat stretch of road, but Jonathan showed strength and superior fitness when faced with a steep hill and reinstated an advantage. On reaching the top of the hill, Jonathan glanced behind; the bullies were still following, so there was little alternative but to head for the woods, which just happened to be but a stone's throw from his friend's house. Once near the wood, Jonathan quickly dismounted and carried his bike and headed for his hiding place where he laid down the bike and covered it with vegetation. Jonathan looked around and listened, he could not see anyone following, but there were the tell tail sounds of cracking twigs and alarm calls from frightened birds, so Jonathan made for the well-hidden trolley and took up his usual position inside, curled up and soon drifted off.

Jonathan had again mysteriously materialised, or at least, his mind had, in a green and pleasant land; he was now known as Egwari who was born in the year 660AD, and the year now was 673AD. Through the doorway of a wooden, framed, thatched building, he was looking out across the Cheviot Hills somewhere in the north of England. Not far from a place called Yeavering, a small but significant settlement, an Anglo-Saxon settlement which was dominated by a very large timber hall. The people who lived at Yeavering were important and governed the area from the large hall, but the family of Egwari did not socialise with those people of such importance, as Egwari was lower in the class system. Now and again, he caught a glimpse of one of the Thegns, a noble warrior who served a prince or king. The family of Egwari farmed the land and took a large portion of their crops to the Hall as a sort of payment, called a tithe, for the privilege of being protected by the Prince; who also owned the land on which they farmed. Egwari did not care too much about working on the small farm and had always enjoyed building things, especially out of stone. On many occasions, Egwari and his friend Cetrick went to the nearby ruins, most likely the remains of Roman buildings and made little camps from the masses of stones laying all around. These two twelve year olds were pretty good at building dry stone walls, which was to be expected as the father of Cetrick was a stonemason called Trelbytuf. Trelbytuf had come over from Gaul to help construct large stone buildings such as churches, monasteries and abbeys. This was the seventh century in England, a time of transformation both in belief and culture, interspersed with occasional conflicts as different Princes and Kings hustled for social importance and land. At the end of one of these so-called building days, Cetrick invited Egwari to his home for some food, and as they sat around fire in the centre of the room, Trelbytuf explained that he had come here at the behest of the Bishop of York. The bishop was a much-travelled man called Wilfrid who had been to Gaul and seen Trelbytuf working on a stone-built abbey and asked him to be part of a gang of stonemasons to construct a new building, a church in the nearby small settlement of Hagustaldes, Bernicia (modern day Hexham in the county of

Northumberland). Knowing that both Egwari and his son, Cetrick, were very enthusiastic when it came to working with stone, Trelbytuf promised to take them, one day soon, to see the whole process. Before setting off for his own family dwelling, Egwari smiled and thanked Trelbytuf for the fresh salmon smeared with honey and served with ample portions of dandelion leaves, borage and fennel. It took Egwari a good hour to arrive back at his family home which was an oblong wooden-framed thatched house with walls constructed from wattle and thickly sealed with daub with a central hearth, where most of the cooking took place. Egwari explained to his family where he had been, what he had done, and what was promised by the father of Cetrick. Both of Egwari's parents were fully aware of his eagerness to work with stone, and Egwari's father, Grantiplis, was keen that a profession as a prospective stonemason could be followed and was very supportive. The mother of Egwari called Goldyfran also thought it a good idea to take advantage of the offer to see how the masons worked and agreed that it could be a better way of life than his father's, who was a hardworking shepherd and farmhand. For the next few days, Egwari helped on the farm, and when Cetrick was seen approaching, Egwari rushed over to greet his good friend, who had news of a visit to Hagustaldes; a settlement that Egwari had only ever been to but once. It was decided that both Cetrick and Egwari would leave the next morning, early enough to travel to Cetrick's home, and from there, take to horseback for the journey down the valley.

In the morrow, there was great excitement as everyone bustled around gathering a few things for the trip to Hagustaldes; things like a blanket for night and a cape for rain. Both Egwari and Cetrick had on their narrow leather belts a *pursa* (small pouch) in which they had five essential herbs: *Borago officinalis* (borage), would give them courage, *Fœniculum* (fennel) for strength, *Urtica urens* (nettle), to protect them from spells, (*Hypericum perforatum*), St. John's wort to drive away demons and last but not least, *Gearwe* (yarrow), to heal any cuts or grazes. In the pursa, there were also a few small coins known as sceattas, just for any emergency. The other item hanging from the belt was a scramasax; this was a small knife that almost everyone carried and could be used for food preparation and anything else that required a sharp blade. Two ponies were sorted out from the farm animals; as Hagustaldes was two days' walk, this would cut down the travelling time by at least a half. It was barely light when they set off, and Grantiplis and Goldyfran waved as the ponies left and wished the two good health and good luck for their journey.

(Now it does bare a thought that once the ponies are out of sight, there is no way to contact or get in touch with the boys; so, imagine going on a journey nowadays without your computer, mobile phone, tablet or any means of sending letters.)

It did not take long to reach the home of Cetrick, and his father was already waiting with his two horses, one horse to ride and the other, his pack-horse, to carry tools and other things. With good weather and a favourable breeze, the band of three should reach Hagustaldes before darkness descended upon the moors. There were some Roman roads still in use, but much of the sixty miles would be across moors and along narrow wooded trackways. It was no race, but it was better if the hut, were the other masons have gathered, could be reached the same day. To keep everyone occupied and happy, Grantiplis recited many old sagas and tales of war and battles of years gone by. One of the more recent being the great battle in 655AD, fought between Penda of the kingdom of Mercia and the hero of Bernicia (part of Northumbria) Oswiu, and the battle was fought at Winwaed. This became one of the favourite stories of the whole trip, and as well as being a story of fearless warriors, it was also a story of a great treasure hidden in the hills to the west of the battle. This was intriguing, as the saga told that the gold and jewels of many mighty sword and dagger pommels were gathered and sent back but disappeared on the way. It was rumoured that some Picts who aided Oswiu during the battle had made off with two saddle bags of bounty, heading westward, and neither the Picts nor the treasure were ever seen again; a story was good for passing time, and the two boys eagerly waited for the next one. Good progress was made, and the travellers had reached the valley of the Harthope Burn (stag valley stream) heading towards Barrowburn; this would be the hardest part of the journey, and there was reassurance from Trelbytuf that things would get better after Barrowburn. There were a few places when all three had to dismount and lead the animals on foot, but nothing that they couldn't handle. A brief rest was welcomed just outside a small shepherd's hovel at Barrowburn, and with the horses watered and rested, they were soon on their way again, along a gentler valley, passing the Blindburn. A keen eye was kept upon any wooded area for there were '*wulf*' (wolves) in most country places, and that was one good reason why the riders were pushing on. They knew the wolves were about for most of the journey by the occasional howls, but they were keeping at a distance. To be in open countryside at night, without shelter, would be to tempt providence, as these creatures would even attack horses, as well as people.

It was not long at all, until they reached the old Roman road called Dere Street, which was straight, flat and well used, and good time was made, even trotting the horses in places. Trelbytuf was determined that the group should be safe and undercover by nightfall; there was good riding all the way to Coriasōpītum, which had been, in its day, one of the largest Roman towns for many miles, from here it was a mere couple of miles to the outskirts of Hagustaldes with just the river Tina (modern day River Tyne) to cross. The travellers reached Coriasōpītum (the meaning of this name could well refer to the old Roman name *Corias* and the Latin word *sōpītum* referring to somewhere quiet or to settle, which could relate to a quiet settlement or a calm, quiet section of river). At twilight, it was decided to camp in the ruins of one of the more substantial Roman buildings rather than travelling in the dark across the tricky ford by Harbottle Island which lead to Hagustaldes. An evening meal of apples, cheese and dried fish was enjoyed by all, and with the horses set to graze, it was time to rest for the night and look forward to the last mile or so in the morning. There was no need of a guard for the horses as the wolves rarely ventured so close to buildings. The morning brought bright sunlight and a good supply of aches and pains from the ride, but they were almost there, and after replenishing the water bags, the group set off along the north bank of the river along a well-trodden path to reach the ford. The river was not high, and at the most about twenty inches deep at this point where a wide stretch of stones formed gentle rapids with an island after fifty yards just about halfway across.

The wolves are at rest but always hungry.

Reaching the south bank, a winding track took them to the bottom of a fairly steep slope rising to a plateau where there stood three large wooden houses and about twenty smaller cottages. More houses than the two youngsters had ever seen in one place. Trelbytuf led them to the nearest of the larger houses and rapped the double-studded oak door with his mason's mallet and, in a load firm voice, let forth the call *frēod, frēod.* This produced the reply *wilcuma frēond,* and the doors were opened wide by a muscular fellow; this was the head mason named Bludigesh who greets Trelbytuf with a warm handshake, who in turn introduced his son, Cetrick and Egwari, as eager apprentices. A servant was sent to take care of the horses, and Bludigesh explained that there was a guest present in the house; none other than Bishop Wilfrid himself along with thirty of the best masons mostly from across the sea. Everyone was crowded around a wooden table looking downwards at a stretched out hide of vellum, on which was drawn the plans of the new church. Each one of those present, apart from Egwari and Cetrick, of course, would be in charge of a team of craftsmen and labourers who had already started to mingle outside. Wilfrid called for silence and produced, from a leather pouch, a small goblet or actually a chalice crafted in glass, and from another pouch poured some water. Lifting the chalice to his lips, Wilfrid took a sip, said a few choice words and sprinkled the remaining few drops across the vellum, therefore, blessing the building, to be. Jonathan recalls that the water was rather foul smelling and later found out that the liquid came from an ancient spring about two miles to the west of Hagustaldes. It was then that the head mason Bludigesh gave orders to those in charge, and Trelbytuf was to be overseer to the supply of stone, for what would be the greatest building that side of the Alps. Egwari and Cetrick would be with the stone gatherers which formed a rather large group of labourers, with many carts and horses. The first task was to construct a new ford across the river, just above Harbottle Island, and already another group was allocated that task. Trelbytuf and the two boys would, along with about fifty workers, be going back to the Roman town of Coriasōpītum in which they had spent the previous night. This would be where the majority of stone would come from, as it was already shaped into good blocks, and all the workers had to do was demolish the buildings and take the stone to the masons at the site of the new church. Every day more and more carts joined the formidable task of transporting thousands of blocks of stone from the Roman structures, the majority of which stood two stories high. Most of the blocks could be carried by two people but some, from the many temples, were twice the size and needed special pulleys to lift them on and off the carts. Back at Hagustaldes, great stacks of stone could be seen in the field, just to the north of the proposed church site. Already some of the original Saxon buildings had been taken down to make way for this new church, and great footings (bases for the walls) had been dug and lined with the larger stones recovered from Coriasōpītum. After a gruelling but enjoyable week dismantling buildings and walls, Trelbytuf informed Egwari and Cetrick that the underground passages and crypt would be constructed before any of the main walls in that area. Cetrick's father would be working on the passages and crypt as he had vast experience in building arches and tunnels, and that this would be the boys' first chance to learn and witness real construction techniques. One good thing, if there was anything they did that was not up to scratch, it would be less noticeable underground than somewhere on the main building. In the meantime, Cetrick and Egwari shared out some of the silver coins (Roman Denarii) and the two gold solidus that they had found during the demolition process. A popular practice was, for those who found them, to attach them to belts and clothing as good luck charms.

There was a rumour circulating through the workers' camp that large platters of silver and an ornate silver goblet had been found near the riverside, and these were presented to Wilfrid to add to his already fantastic collection of treasures and saintly artefacts that would be displayed in the church, once finished. The next morning, the belts were displayed proudly, each with a dozen shiny silver coins riveted to the leather, and truly a shining example of craftsmanship, but for what purpose Jonathan inquires. These are the things that memories are made of; these are the inanimate objects that make possessions but most often possess your very thoughts to the extent that all too often they can control your actions. Possessions are the beginning of inward views of life when things should be shared, like food or water and not clung too. There will come a time when you are surrounded by possessions, and they can act as chains and burdens which rule your life; discard any possession that serves as a memory (for memories are in the mind), and live for the future and not the past. The belts, of course, keep things together, keep things tight, but adornments serve little use at all. Over the next few weeks, the crypt took form and many passages lead in various directions, some could be described as tunnels, and one in particular descended by steps many hundreds of yards to the flat fields by the river. This tunnel was used as an alternative access for supplies brought in by boats and would be closed when the church was completed. The tunnel also had side rooms, lined with fine stone and kept solely for the purpose of storing Wilfrid's collection of wondrous things whilst the building work proceeded. Both Cetrick and Egwari were now shaping stones with narrow-bladed iron chisels, with the masons themselves doing the actual building. One of the most interesting things was the number of stones that contained Roman writing on their faced sides; not that the writing could be read by Egwari, but it was looked upon as something mysterious; even more so when working in the flickering light of an oil lamp. The lamps were only used in the darkness of the tunnels as the main work on the rooms of the crypt were in full daylight; that was until the walls started to arch over and the ceilings began to form when the crypt walls reach two yards in height which would be about ground level for the main floors. The next week would again be backward and forward between the church and Coriasōpītum, for now the outside walls had begun to rise from the footings and head for the sky, like towering giants.

There was no conservation orders or governing bodies such as 'English Heritage' or 'Historic England' and no listed buildings in those days as any older unused buildings were at the mercy of stone gatherers to use on anything from cow byers to great churches. So when all the Romans had left this island by 410AD.to defend their borders, there was a lot of nicely-hewn stone for the taking.

Wilfrid had gone back to the monastery at Ripon where another church had been planned and left the building plans with Bludigesh who, by now, was fashioning fine window mouchettes and mouldings pleasing to the eye. In the evenings, when work was finished, there could be heard the tap, tap, tap of the mallets wielded by the hands of Cetrick and Egwari as they practiced the art of stone carving, trying to match the mastery of Bludigesh. Realising that it would take many mountains of stone and a multitude of days to reach an acceptable result the two trainees, after glancing at the accumulated pile of chippings from their efforts, retired for the night. There were thoughts of their families back in the hills, and no doubt, their families were wondering how their offspring were progressing in their prospective new occupations. In those days, there was no minimum age limit to working, and as there was no such thing as a benefit system when a child was fit enough to work and add an income to a household, then so be it.

The noise of carts and horses awaken the workers as more help arrived, some friendly Picts from the border regions, and there was much talk of three large barges coming down the river to help transport the stones recovered from Coriasōpītum. Grabbing their cart and accompanied by two young brothers, Bebelumbe and Shappergors, who had come all the way from Gaul, now pals of Egwari and Cetrick, they all joined a caravan of carts. As they reached the newly-constructed ford, they could see the new barges, one of which laden piled high with worked stone and already, even this early in the day, being unpacked and stacked. The other barges were seen just turning a bend in the river and empty; they looked like large fish serving platters but 40 yards in length with upwards sloping prows and sterns. These had been built as copies of Roman river transport barges of which two had been found in the silts of the river nearer to the coast, not far from the monastery of St. Hilda. These barges held more than ten carts worth of stones, but the carts had the advantage of delivering the stones very near the church boundary. Each barge was able to make three round trips per day, and between the carts and the barges, a huge stockpile of good stone had grown outside of the walls of the church. There was a constant background sound of mallets upon chisels, chisels upon stone, carts rumbling, horses neighing, and above all that, the calls of masons and labourers could be heard.

Two months had gone by, and the finishing touches to the crypt or almost done, a job which had taken seven masons, four apprentices, fourteen labourers and many hundreds of stone blocks to complete. The ceilings of the crypt are now just below ground level, and Cetrick along with Egwari, carrying flaming torches headed along one of the passageways leading north and into one of the side chambers they had helped to build, with the objective of removing any rubble. A shock awaited them when entering the chamber, a small oil lamp was in a recess, and three heads turned to face them, and it was Wilfrid himself along with a musician who was called Aedde Stephen or Eddius Stephenus and another person unknown. As the lights of the larger torches illuminated the scene, there could be seen wondrous things glinting and sparkling in the flickering light. A great chest of silver platters, goblets a plenty and a small pyramid of Roman silver coins. Wilfrid had seen and spoken to the young apprentices before and had seen them hard at work in the crypt; Wilfrid made a sign and thanked the two trainees for their efforts, and that they should be gratified with the accomplishment adding some words; which are recalled here by Jonathan, '*remember this, young person, great things are built of stone, but greater things are built of wisdom*'. Egwari explained their presence, and the three dignitaries left accordingly to allow the work to be done with departing words of '*leave not a light behind you, but follow the light that leads'.* The clean-up did not take long at all, and with only a few stray rough edges to smooth out the passageway room, was finished. Only one last thing to do, and that was to put a mason's mark on a stone that Egwari had trimmed and smoothed; the mark that was to be seen on the lower right of the chamber entrance is from the early Anglo-Saxon alphabet called the *Elder Futhark* and represents the letter 'E'. (This does look like an 'M' but would be pronounced as an 'E'; in this alphabet an 'M' looks like two pennants facing each other). All carts would be back to Coriasōpītum, and the sight of near forty carts being pulled by two horses each was not too be missed. The carts lined up next to one of the Roman granaries which was near five yards in height, ninety-eight yards in length and with well-cut stones all the way, this would be rich pickings. Three of the carts were piled high with oblong slabs from pavements and monuments, some depicting Roman inscriptions and representations of Roman gods; all to be used for church construction purposes. One of these carts had become a little unbalanced, and just as it passed midway along the ford, over it went. The whole cartload of stone slabs fell into the river, which at that point was about 36 inches deep; there was shouting and yelling as everyone tried to save the labourer who was riding on top of the slabs, but the poor person was trapped under many tonnes, and there was little hope. The slabs had been loaded by using a hoist, and without a hoist, there was no means to move them, and they were left where they fell, labourer and all. The wheels were recovered from the cart, and the unhurt horses freed from their harnesses; what was left of the cart was pushed into the river to float away, and the stones left as a monument to the worker. As with all construction work, there is an element of risk so accidents are a reality and an occupational hazard that is almost inevitable, and all the workers were aware that concentration and an awareness of safety was essential. It took further two weeks to dismantle this granary which, in its day, held stores of grain and foodstuffs enough to feed the soldiers along the Roman Wall and the garrison of this once large town.

Great arches began to appear as the magnificent church reached half its height and the scaffolding grew ever higher and higher reaching for the sky; what a sight. Egwari with Cetrick and the two brothers, Bebelumbe and Shappergors, had been selected, as a team, to follow the master masons making sure that the stones to be used were clean of all defects, any old mortar removed and of a regular size.

After work on this particular day, the group of four decided to venture into the newly-constructed crypt just to show Bebelumbe and Shappergors the tunnels and side chambers; so torches were lit, and in they went. Just about one hundred and ten yards along the longest tunnel they arrive at the chamber where Egwari had met Wilfrid and Stephenus, but now the chamber was not to be seen as the entrance had been blocked. The stonework used to conceal the chamber, matched the rest of the tunnel, and they could just define where the arched entrance had once been. It appeared that the treasures of Wilfrid had been protected, and few knew of its existence. Back they went to the lodgings, disappointed not to have shown their handiwork but intrigued nonetheless. Egwari and Cetrick wondered if they would ever see the room they built ever again.

The mason's mark of Egwari.

The next few days were long and hard as many tonnes of stone were transported by both barge and cart and great logs of oak began to arrive, cut down from nearby woods in readiness for making the many beams of the roof. Now that most of the stone required had been stacked, the apprentices could concentrate on learning to carve both intricate designs and sculptures that would eventually be used on the walls of the sanctuary. Many hours turned into many days which, in turn, merged into weeks, during which time Egwari and Cetrick had become quite skilled at carving anything from delicate vines to faces.

Jonathan adds that there was a kind of satisfaction (not pride) in watching things grow and develop with the realisation that they would last for hundreds of years and be admired by thousands of people. It was also pleasing for the mind that he was being taught skills that not long ago were not only unthinkable but also unattainable.

Egwari had just completed his tenth animal carving when in the workshop walked Bludigesh who made a beeline for Egwari and explained that because he was pleased with the work on the sculptures, as a consequence Wilfrid had a special job for him. Cetrick would finish the carvings for the sanctuary, and Egwari would carve the coffin lid for the young worker called Syfelldam who drowned when the cart overturned on the ford. Syfelldam happened to be the son of a Thegn, named Fymyla, who had been allocated to protect Wilfred from bandits during Wilfrid's travels. Fymyla was the mysterious third person that Cetrick and Egwari had seen briefly in the chamber of treasures before the doorway was blocked up. Apparently, The Thegn saw a resemblance, in Egwari, to his son and had requested Wilfrid that it would be fitting if another young person could have the honour of carving the lid. Egwari agreed to the task and added that it would be a privilege to take the task and with the help of Trelbytuf selected a large block of stone to form the lid. The stone slab was recovered during low water levels, one of the very same that had tumbled from the ill-fated cart that weeks ago had tipped over and trapped the hapless Syfelldam. With the assistance of Cetrick, Trelbytuf and Bebelumbe, the large slab was lifted into the workshop, and Egwari immediately started to chip away at the stone, and from an oblong slab, turned it into a more stretched oval shape. That was the easy bit now for the design Egwari chose because they were building a church, a form of cross, a cross that would be unique. Egwari had only seen a handful of crosses and chose a simple design with three short arms atop of a longer body, and the four ends formed to match the paddles used to propel the barges that were used to transport, along with the carts, the many thousands of stones from Coriasōpītum. After six or seven sketches, the final design was scratched onto the coffin lid. This would be a raised design, so Egwari chipped away until an outline could be seen, and that was enough for that day. That evening, Egwari told the story of the coffin lid to his friends who were very interested and really impressed that a worker would be honoured in this way and offered to carry the lid when the time came. They would have great difficulty in carrying the coffin like they do in the present day, as it was made of solid stone, and not even six the size and strength of Bludigesh would be capable of that. The next morning Egwari could not wait to complete the lid and was up with the lark chipping away with his mallet and chisel. A simple but effective design standing proud of the lid and the shadows, casted from the light from a window, enhanced the outline adding a certain air of serenity. The actual coffin itself was hewn from a plain block of stone; already set in position. A short inscription was chiselled either side of the cross of the lid, reading 'PIA MEMORIA, SYFDM' (in memory Syfelldam) and a delicately carved Chi Rho as a centrepiece. The end product looked good, and Egwari was satisfied with his efforts; the only concern was would Fymyla be happy with the outcome.

It was late in the day when Fymyla finally arrived at the workshop to inspect the lid and was most pleased with the workmanship of Egwari. This would actually be the first burial inside the new church, and prior to the flagstones being laid just one foot above the coffin, forming the completed floor; once the roof was finished, of course. The service was arranged and was to be performed by none other than Wilfrid himself, and the lid laid as a final farewell to a young soul remembered. There was a good gathering for the service, and all there knew in the hearts that it could have been any one of the workers that succumbed to an accident. Wilfred said a few words and raised his small glass chalice as a toast and blessing to the young life and explained that this very chalice was normally used only for sacraments, and that this would be the first and most likely the last time it would be used during funerary rites. The stone lid, displaying the rood (cross), was placed ceremoniously atop the coffin, and plans were already in place to section this area off by a screen once the floors had been laid. This screen and any carvings to adorn that place had been already allocated to be constructed and carved by Trelbytuf, father of Egwari. After the service, Fymyla approached Egwari and took from a leather purse the most beautiful relic holder; this was about 9 inches in height and called a feretory; passed it to Egwari as a reward for the coffin lid. The next day, everything and everyone carried on as before, and Wilfrid, because of the great amount of stone still piled high unused and surplus to requirements, decided to build other smaller churches; one a stone's throw away but dedicated to a different saint. Another small church was to be built on the island of Lindisfarne for the monk Cuthbert, who had heard of the building of the great church at Hagustaldes; this would not take long at all just being about eight yards in total length; consisting of just a nave and chancel with a thatched roof.

An excellent idea as all the workmen were still here and with an increasing number of benefactors, money was no problem. There was much talk between the two brothers Shappergors and Bebelumbe who had met up with Cetrick and Egwari concerning the treasures of the hidden crypt, and indeed, if they were still there. Some of the items were on display in the main church, but there were no signs of the large number of Roman silver plates, goblets, platters and the pyramid of silver coins. Of course, the matter had little to do with the workers, but it was just out of curiosity, but it was not a question that could be asked of Wilfred, Fymyla or even Eddius Stephenus and so would probably remain a mystery for many years to come. One rumour that had been circulating the camp was that the warriors of tribes fighting in the west could be passing through on their way back to the far north, and that was the reason for the hidden chamber in the crypt tunnel being blocked up.

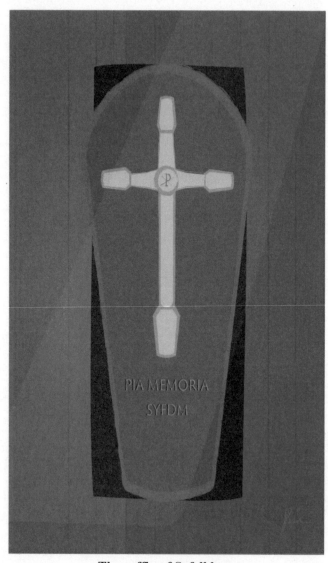

The coffin of Syfelldam.

It was decided by Trelbytuf to return to home for a while before starting the rood screen carvings, just to make sure that everything was alright and come back after a week; both of his charges Egwari and Cetrick would accompany him on the journey. The return journey would again be on horseback and may take two days because a great deal of the route would be uphill as they head north to the Cheviots. They set off the next day after saying farewell to the other workers and added that in a few days they would return. The easiest part came first this time as they followed the Roman road Dere Street from the old Roman town of Coriasōpītum for approximately 30 miles. The very same town from which, for many months, large quantities of good stone were taken to build Wilfrid's church at Hagustaldes. This first part had taken seven hours and still had the hard part to negotiate as they headed towards the Blindburn. The undergrowth and vegetation had grown somewhat, and with 7 miles to go to a suitable resting place at Barrowburn, a decision was made by Trelbytuf to camp for the night as soon as they reached the old buildings and shepherds hut at Barrowburn. Just about halfway to the shepherds hut, two riders approached in the opposite direction; they were from a clan little further north, Votadini from the kingdom of Brynaich and not at all trustworthy. There was an exchange of greetings and a few questions from the Votadini, all a little nervy, and Trelbytuf appeared a little relieved as they went on their way. By evening, the hut was reached, and the horses were stabled; it was a very demanding journey, a lot tougher than the last time they passed through, in part due to the seemingly never-ending uphill climbs. With horses and riders, most of the second half of the journey because of the tough terrain was actually on foot. It was late morning on the second day when the intrepid travellers reached dense woodland approaching the start of Harthope Burn when, suddenly and without warning, they were surrounded by a dozen or so Votadini. One dismounted and approached Trelbytuf and gave his name as Cripnoos, and this painted warrior explained that this group was from the north and had been fighting with the tribes of Cymru. Cripnoos wished no harm to the travellers but needed the horses and whatever Trelbytuf's party was carrying, but they could keep their swords as goodwill and a protection from the wolf packs in the area. Outnumbered and within a day's walk from home, there was little to gain from extended bargaining and so agreed with the request. (Jonathan recounts that he was more than a little scared for their safety but stood firm and upright against adversity). A request was made by Egwari to keep his pouch as it contained a gift and memory of a friend who died at work and showed the feretory to Cripnoos. The Votadini warrior handled the gift but took a liking to it and politely denied the request but showed gratitude by leaving food and drink for the travellers and left as silently as they came.

Trelbytuf, Cetrick and Egwari all agreed that the situation could have been a lot worse, and they were thankful that they had their shoes let alone their lives. With just about 6 miles to go and with no baggage to carry, the distance was covered quickly and with three hours of daylight left. Egwari let out a call *hālettan frið hāl*, and out of the wooden shack rushed his mother Goldyfran following close behind his father Grantiplis. Hugs and greetings all around, and an invite to Trelbytuf and Cetrick to spend the night before returning to their home was accepted. There was a cry from inside the shack, and there in the back of the room could be seen a crib. Goldyfran lifted out a small baby and introduced to Egwari his new sister Daphi. Well, there was a lot to catch up on, and the evening was nonstop talking, and no doubt the tales would continue for many days to come. The morning arrived quickly with all parties fully refreshed, even though the night was spent mainly in conversation with no one, apart from Daphi having much sleep. Farewells were said to Cetrick and his father, Trelbytuf, both would return in a week to travel back to Hagustaldes, and hopefully, new horses would be found for the journey. That was the last time Jonathan remembers being in Northumberland, building churches or dodging Votadini warriors. As Jonathan awoke from the shopping trolley, he mentioned that tears were in his eyes, not from pain but from the separation from a life that he actually enjoyed.

There was a sense of accomplishment in carving and being part of constructing something that would outlast not only his lifetime but many, many generations. A tingle of awareness that life was about leaving a legacy behind, and in doing so, the pleasure derived from both teaching others and learning new skills is the personal reward.

The feretory made of gold and silver.

It is almost as if it was preordained in the human gene bank to learn, as if it was the universe requesting knowledge from lifeforms in the progression of the cosmos. The recollections of Jonathan infers that this was one of the most rewarding lifeways he has experienced and will remember the great walls of the church reaching, as if they were outstretched arms towards the sky and described the whole as awesome. The loss of the feretory was regrettable, but Jonathan was pragmatic in so much that it was an object, and that the memory was greater than the object itself because the memory lives on. A personal memento, in the form of an object, is nothing more than a manifestation of materialism which is one of the downfalls of humanity. Jonathan realised this and became more inclined to discard thoughts and objects that could not be benefitted from, either as a collective learning or teaching tool.

Of interest is that both, the crypt in the Northumbrian town of Hexham and the ruins of the Roman town of Coriasōpītum (Corstopitum) are still there to be seen, to this very day.

Jonathan again makes his way home wondering how he had lived, worked and experienced many months in little more than just twenty minutes.

One explanation could be autobiographical memories known as 'Life-Review Experiences' (LRE) which are usually stored in areas like the parietal, medial temporal and the prefrontal cortices of the human brain. This, of course, would only relate to memories of a single lifetime, so the possibility remains that memories of previous lifetimes are stored somewhere in human DNA and actual genes handed down over millennia. Every one of us has hidden away, not only a history but also histories of many lifetimes, past present and future; mark my words for these are the truths. Think of the modern storage devises, so small, yet containing such unbelievable amounts of information, and only then will you realise the power of DNA, an atom of which contains worlds unseen and adventures unknown.

With a quick look around, Jonathan realises the coast is clear and makes a dash for home, to bed and a chance to reflect on the experiences, that are so real, so vibrant that surely, according to Jonathan, must have been a physical, factual, genuine existence.

Chapter 7
The Stars, the Sun and the Sail

Characters: Poccabeady, Beachcampken, Ifauflogmen, Capcifi, Cattalin, Intcaract, Ninida, Otiunderstars, Stoneyrama, Saramemara, Chairanseat, Croozefeast, Arthenos.

It was a rainy day with the school week finished, and Jonathan had thoughts of relaxing on the riverbank because the hatching of the mayfly coupled with a drop of rain meant that the trout and seatrout would be feeding. Out comes the fly box, and Jonathan sorts through the three dozen or so flies he has handmade, one for every occasion and pulls out most likely to attract some fish for the table. With the rain, maybe the bullies will be indoors and dry rather than chasing shadows around the countryside. As well as being with friends and participating in enjoyable pastimes; one of the most pleasurable things is to be in the company of oneself and enjoying a hobby that advocates sometimes solitude is a benefit. It would appear that fly fishing is one such hobby that falls into this category as there is a sort of oneness with nature; almost a form of meditation with water as a mesmerising agent and an activity, amongst others, that even brings a smile to the face by the very thought of taking part. Jonathan looks upon this day as one to remember, not only because he enjoyed himself but as one of the, infrequent, days that the bullies did not mar; albeit, there were many a glance over the shoulder, almost anticipating the appearance of the bullies. A couple of days later, Jonathan recalls one of the most painful and harrowing of encounters, burnt into the very soul, injecting fear that is etched into the memory as if for a lifetime. Jonathan was taking part in the school cross-country race, something that he had mastered and excelled at, as it seemed he had spent a large part of his childhood and early youth running away from adversity. Not far from finish of this four mile run and leading by about fifty yards, Jonathan enters a small copse and is tripped by an outstretched leg. Over he went and is suddenly grabbed by the feet by three bullies who took his running shoes and gleefully repeatedly dragged him backward and forward through a dense patch of vicious stinging nettles; they run off laughing, with the shoes as a prize. There, left in a heap and shaking with fear and pain with a myriad of red blotches from head to foot, Jonathan stands; he looks to the heavens and shouts 'why me? Why me?' One of the other runners stops to ask if he is OK, Jonathan nods and sets off with a bucketful of determination, grit and adrenalin; with no regard for pain and bare feet. He eventually crosses the finish line in third place and in doing so, makes the county team; his feet look a mess covered in a mixture of mud and blood from the many cuts sustained from running bare-footed. His feet are washed by the P.E. teacher who asks what happened. All Jonathan could say is that he lost his shoes in the mud of a burn and stumbled into a bed of nettles. The teacher finds a spare pair of plimsolls and gives them to Jonathan, who, by now, looks a sorry sight with; face, arms and legs exploding in colour from the stings and heads for home a little worse for wear. Lo and behold, there they are again waiting at the top of the road blocking the way to his street and moving towards Jonathan, who recalls thinking 'they are not going to catch me again today' and takes off like the wind. In hot pursuit, the bullies give chase, but Jonathan can run, boy; he can run. He reaches the woods and the refuge, which is still well-hidden in the dense undergrowth and curls inside the shopping trolley actually trembling like a leaf in a storm (sometimes, anticipations of life are overshadowed by reality). Jonathan brings to mind a tune he had heard on the radio, a tune that brings teardrops to his weary eyes, drops that caress his cheeks as a warm tickle; the tune by Domenico Zipoli is called *'Elevazione',* and soon young Jonathan drifts again, to another time, another place.

Before even opening his eyes, Jonathan could smell the sea in the breeze a salted aroma of seaweed, feel the gentle swell and drop of the waves, hear general chatter and the sound of wind in the flapping sails. It is early morning as he drops from his hammock to the cabin's floor and at over six foot tall is slightly stooped under the cabin roof. His name is now Cattalin, who is an experienced and respected deckhand on board, a small seagoing vessel along with eight other crew members. The weather is fair, and the sea gentle in its tranquillity. The ship looks like a fishing boat but trimmed lean for speed, and it looks majestic as it cuts the waves powered by a gentle south-easterly breeze. As he mounts the short steps to the deck, Cattalin takes a long deep breath of his beloved sea air; almost as an elixir, the salt air gives the breather a magical lift just like a glass of good wine. He greets fellow sailor Otiunderstars, a Swedish navigator, a person of untold knowledge of those things that twinkle in the sky; about whom is said that he has never been lost; but maybe, at times, he just doesn't know where he is. The crew are in good spirits as they near the coastline of Spain from where they will collect a cargo of barrels or tubs, as they are generally known, containing some of the best brandies which they will then sell, once the ship returns to the Isle of Man. The name of the ship 'Spanish Head' is just a coincidence and has little to do with its destination because the ship actually takes its name from the spit of land found near the harbour where it was built on the Isle of Man. There is a local rumour that many years ago a ship from the ill-fated Spanish Armada had sank just off the coast of the Isle of Man, and that spit of land from that very day has been known as 'Spanish Head'.

This was not a pirate ship but a fishing vessel used as a means of transporting goods for those who are willing to pay. The Spanish Head is a ship used for the age old profession of 'smuggling', an occupation enjoyed by some and shared by many. The ship anchored up, two hundred yards from the shore, just inside a small calm bay, and the cook, Croozefeast, got to work and soon produced a masterpiece comprising many different seafood delicacies washed down with good ale; this is good living. All would sleep well that night, and in the hour before dawn, a small lamp will be lit to signify that the crew is ready to receive the cargo. A distant light signalled the all clear and the shore party comprising of: 'Intcaract', the Bosun, who is a shrewd and capable negotiator, 'Beachcampken', who is a strong, alert and reliable shipmate, and there are no worries when he is covering the transfer, Ifauflogmen, a strong-minded, silent type renowned for his swimming ability and with Cattalin, boarded a small rowing boat. The sea was calm, and it took little more than five minutes before hauling the rowing boat to the

147

safety of the high water mark. Intcaract and Ifauflogmen silently disappeared through dense sea grass onto the dunes of steep golden, sand and it was not long before the all-clear was signalled. With Beachcampken guarding the boat, Cattalin joined the advance party and following a meandering path through grass and gorse for near on a mile, to arrive at a small hamlet where the negotiations would take place in the rear room of an unpretentious house. This Hamlet was familiar to Cattalin as he was born and brought up not many miles away, until the age of thirteen when he, at that age, was expected to earn and contribute to the household. Cattalin knew all of the inhabitants of the hamlet, especially his childhood friend 'Saramemara' (I notice a sparkle in the eyes of Jonathan and a wry grin upon his face); apparently, they were inseparable from an early age, and Cattalin looked forward to seeing her beautiful smile again. So, while Intcaract and Beachcampken meet and barter with the suppliers, Cattalin headed for familiar surroundings.

The negotiations began with the entrance of Ninida (who happened to be the grandmother of Saramemara) and a formidable exponent of the technique of bargaining and one who knew everything there was to know about tubs, brandy and life; 'to deal in something, one must know its worth, and to know its worth, you have to make it' is a moral that fits the bill here. The extended family of Ninida has, for generation after generation, made barrels and tubs for the brandy industry. Beachcampken, along with a couple of the villagers, would make sure the talks, which could take anything from thirty minutes or six hours, are not interrupted; until all the details are ironed out *de acuerdo.*

Saramemara lived in a prime position overlooking the rest of the small village, and as Cattalin strides up the steep approach, there was a sense of homecoming and the familiar surroundings that made his heart flutter in anticipation. The wooden shutters of the house were open, and the heavy scent of Hibiscus thick in the air was an added bonus to the splendid multi-coloured display. On nearing the door, which was ajar, Cattalin emitted a whistle (learnt from his shipmate, Stoneyrama, who is a native of the Canary Islands, the inhabitants of which use this whistling language called *El Silbo*), a sound all too familiar to Saramemara. When, within seconds, a vision of loveliness appeared in the flickering shadows of the doorway; a beauty emanating like light from a torch putting the magnificence of the blooming Hibiscus to shame. Attired in a bright red bodice and a dress of sky blue and grass green, her hair pulled into a neat bun, highlighting her tanned skin framing the largest pair of hazel eyes as if set in huge white pearls. Beauty, indeed, is not only in the eye of the beholder but also in the memory of those who have been apart. A warm greeting ensued and Cattalin called Saramemara by a pet name *mariposa* meaning a butterfly. Cattalin had been at sea, this trip, for two months; in fact, he had been at sea for over two years but returned to his birth country whenever possible, mainly to see his fiancée. In those two years, Cattalin had saved his share of monies in a ceramic pot kept in a small recess at the bottom of Saramemara's kitchen wall, protected by a removable brick. This fund was to be used for the couple's wedding which had been planned for over four years. Saramemara still lived with her Grandmother Ninida, and the couple were also expected to continue to live there. This was the goal of the two sweethearts, a true love that had grown since childhood in mutual expectation, passion and commitment.

The parents of Saramemara had, for many years, been involved with exporting top quality brandy, but they were lost in an unfortunate accident when their transfer boat hit rocks whilst escaping the dreaded customs men. All were fully aware of the perils involved, but it (smuggling) was a way of life and a means of survival for this tight knit community.

It is often said that a humble life of 'peace and quiet' is better than a splendid one filled with danger, but needs require action, and action, by its very nature, involves risks. Danger and adversity are things that cannot always be avoided, but the way we handle the situation is a skill, a skill that is often an automatized cognitive action.

There was no thought to the progress of the meeting taking place in the village below as this was a process that had taken place many times before and really was little more than a customary formality. As Saramemara looked dearly into the eyes of her beloved, as if minds spoke without words, Saramemara sank slowly into the willing, loving arms of Cattalin, her betrothed; they kiss passionately.

Saramemara greets Cattalin.

Gently the two lovers sank to the floor, and beneath the warmth of the bread oven enjoyed their love; there was no guilt; this was just living a life in a time when coupled with much uncertainty owing to a truly dangerous occupation and 'the moment' is all. Now cradled in each other's arms, they smiled into eyes that sparkled like miniature supernovas; the memory of what just took place, burnt into their very souls for eternity. Two hours had elapsed by the time Ninida returned with the news that an amicable decision had been reached which was good news all round. Unfortunately, Ninida had forgotten to put the bread in the oven before the meeting, but a quick thinking Saramemara, helped by Cattalin, made sure there was a bun in the oven for Ninida to enjoy. The next couple of days would see forty tubs of the best brandy transported from the warehouses to the secret floors of the ship. Until then, time was for relaxation for the crew as the guards around the village would make sure that there were no strangers' eyes looking in the wrong direction. Ninida was happy to see the couple so in love; she smiled broadly at something that had brought back the memory of her husband, who, for fifty years, masterminded the supply of brandy to the smuggling ships.

The tubs mysteriously appeared during the third night; nothing was heard, nothing was seen; they just silently arrived in the darkness. Samples were taken, just to make sure the contents were true, and the quality was good. The ship had a false bottom, like another floor, accessible only through a hatch located below the Spanish Head's oven, and it took most of the day to load and secure the cargo. The plan was to leave the next morning, as it did not pay to be too long in one place and kept that one step ahead of, not only the opposition but also the custom's men. Ninida rustled up a giant paella for all the crew, the aroma of which must have drifted through the hills for miles. The music, supplied by the locals, was out of this world; there were three *vihuelas* (a form of guitar), two pipers playing on Galician *gaitas* (like a small bagpipe), three double reed *gralla* (an early form of flute), two experts of the *flabiol* and *tambori* (combined flute and drum). All these musicians created a truly enchanting almost magical sound, and accompanied by several dancers swirling in unison, their castanets rhythmically echoing into the night. As the night wore on and nearly all were (apart from Ninida who's pleasure came from watching everyone else enjoying themselves), feeling the effects of the local wine. Cattalin was handed the *flabiol* and *tambori* which he had played before; up stood Saramemara who had borrowed a set of castanets and joined the dancers.

In the eyes of Jonathan I could see tears begin to form (it is hard to differentiate between whether the emotions felt were extreme happiness or deepest sorrow) as he tells me of a special dance, a dance he associates with a love, a love once known. At times like this, I can sympathise with Jonathan, who must have lived many lives, lives he remembers in detail and with feelings, but these are only part lives, mere snapshots of a whole; the tale continues.

Cattalin handed back the *flabiol* and *tambori* and took the hand of his beloved '*Mariposa*', and together they (the lovers) performed a magnificent Bolero, full of passion, moving as one, in time to the sharp hand-clapping and the triple time of the duelling vihuelas. Cheers filled the air as they flung back their heads and raised their left arms towards the moon at the end of that rustic rendition, radiating a roguish reality. What a memorable evening plucked from many hundreds of ordinary days when life 'just goes on'; as yet another day consumed by the sense of merely existing.

That evening the whole village slept soundly, peacefully, and an air of contentment shrouded the hamlet like an unseen mist; only the guards could be seen silhouetted against a pale blueish sky; a sky full of stars, love, hope and expectations.

The next morning saw the final preparations before sailing, as another thirty tubs were loaded onto the Spanish Head, but this time, the tubs were completely empty. These would act as a decoy in the cargo held above the false floor; this floor was the creation of the ship's carpenter who went by the apt name of Chairanseat, a master of the axe and saw. If the ship was stopped by the custom's patrol or anyone else for that matter, the crew would say that they were transporting empty barrels from the makers to the wine merchants of France, and the paperwork that the ship carried would match the ruse. It was still dusk as the sailor's waved their farewells, and soon the boat was heading for the open sea and blessed with a steady breeze and gentle swell. Keeping the land just in sight, the Spanish Head would hug the coastline until it reached France and the small harbour of St. Nazaire, where they would pick up a legitimate cargo of wine; this be entered into the ship's log which they would declare if need be. Two days into the journey it was quite noticeable that Ifauflogmen had developed, unlike him, a habit of just eating half of his meal and taking the rest away, apparently for later. Just another day to go before they reached the small port of St. Nazaire, and Stoneyrama, who had been on watch high in the rigging, slid down the masthead rope to inform the captain Capcifi that a large ship had been trailing them for the last three hours. There was more than a little suspiciousness amongst the crew, as a ship of that size should be more than capable of overtaking the Spanish Head, but there it was about two miles off the stern, intriguing indeed. Capcifi gave the command to alter course twenty degrees north north-west and head out to sea.

The evening was setting in, and everyone came on the deck, and it was unnerving to see that the larger vessel had also altered their course following the Spanish Head; something was indeed afoot. Coming into the French harbour of St. Nazaire, the crew felt as if they had reached a sanctuary, a refuge from the eyes of the follower, and all were relieved as the larger vessel did not follow them into the harbour but anchored out at sea, almost purposefully, just on the horizon. That evening, after a meal on board, Capcifi spoke to the whole crew and (although to be followed was not an unusual occurrence for smugglers) informed the crew that evasive action could well be on the agenda. Both Cattalin and Otiunderstars were asked to join the captain atop deck, where a glass of rum awaited, to discuss the various options available. Knowing that the Spanish Head would be anchored in the safe harbour of St. Nazaire for only two days and three nights, plans needed to be finalised, in readiness for immediate evasive action. The next morning, during the delivery of thirty barrels of excellent wine, enquiries were made about the large ship anchored on the horizon, and all that could be found out was that the very same ship had been seen sailing up and down the coast for the past two weeks. The paperwork was handed over, and the barrels were secured, and the plan was to wait for the later tide and set sail halfway through the 'Middle Watch' about two o'clock in the morning, in darkness, just as four bells sounded.

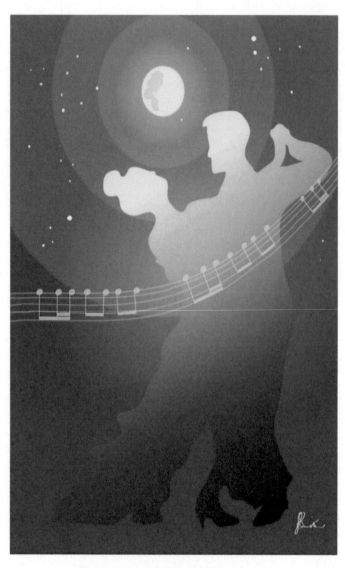

The two lovers dance the Bolero.

Capcifi sent Poccabeady, who, as well as a deckhand, was a sailmaker AKA 'The Stitcher', up the masts to check all the sails in readiness for the planned night maneuverers. Poccabeady finished the inspection which found nothing that needed urgent attention and then grabbed a few morsels of food before settling into a comfortable hammock to catch four hours sleep in readiness for his turn on watch, the 'Middle Watch'.

Jonathan enlightens me of the complexities of both the ships watches and bell tolling which sounded like a well-drilled routine, a routine now imprinted upon his very soul.

A Ship's Watch:

First Watch	8pm to midnight
Middle Watch	midnight to 4am
Morning Watch	4am to 8am
Forenoon	8am to noon
Afternoon	noon to 4pm
First Dog Watch	4pm to 6pm
Second Dog Watch	6pm to 8pm

The Ship's Bells:

A ship will only have one bell which is rung every half hour, and the number of rings is determined by the chart below. After the first half an hour from the start of each watch and every half hour of the watch followed, more rings or bells and short pauses shown as (p). Each watch is four hours long apart from the 'Dog Watches' which, because of meal times, are only two hours in length.

Half hour	1 bell.
One hour	2 bells
One and a half	2 bells (p) 1 bell.
Two hours	2 bells (p) 2 bells.
Two and a half	2 bells (p) 2 bells (p) 1 bell.
Three hours	2 bells (p) 2 bells (p) 2 bells.
Three and a half	2 bells (p) 2 bells (p) 2 bells (p) 1 bell.
Four hours	2 bells (p) 2 bells (p) 2 bells. (p) 2 bells

The latter is commonly known in nautical circles as eight bells, indicating both the end of the watch and beginning of the next watch. Unless, of course, the watch ending is one of the short 'Dog Watches' which ends with four bells.

The Spanish Head would sail south, back down the coast until they were completely out of sight of the large vessel and then head due west at full sail before turning north to head home and the Isle of Man. This would only happen if the night was clear so that Otiunderstars could plot and follow the course using the night sky as his guide. The 'First Watch' would be Cattalin, and starting at 2000hrs, the watch would be completed in four hours at eight bells midnight, then just two hours sleep before all hands would be on deck and full sail ahoy. Just as Cattalin climbed the short wooden stairs to the main deck, he spotted a shadow at the top of the stairs; it turned out to be Ifauflogmen carrying a small package waiting to descend the steps. Greetings were passed, and both expressed that the excitement of eluding the large ship was something to look forward to and bade a good night to each other. Cattalin assumed that Ifauflogmen had, inside the small package, food to eat in isolation as he had been accustomed to do since leaving the haven of the Spanish hamlet. No questions asked, or indeed needed, as Cattalin, being a well-travelled seafarer, was well aware that people had different habits as individuals, and the only time to question anyone was when there was danger to either the ship or the rest of the crew, and eating a morsel of food away from the main table was nothing to worry about. The four hours flew by, and Cattalin handed over to Poccabeady, who arrived just as the eight bells had tolled. It is amazing how the brain acts as an alarm clock; even when asleep, the grey matter counts the bells and signals the eyes to open. As four bells rang out, everyone came on deck awake and alert for the task ahead, and as there were only three hours of darkness left, everyone knew their pre-arranged positions. The tide had just started to ebb as the Spanish Head glided silently out of the harbour, and there would be no more bells rung or fires lit that night. A little more than a gentle breeze propelled the ship at a leisurely four knots as it made its way south back down the coast, until the large ship was out of sight; then full sail. The skies were mostly clear, allowing Otiunderstars to plot the course as Capcifi kept the telescope trained on the large ship as two hours had passed, and only the crows-nest of the other vessel could be seen as the skies begin to brighten; all should be well. Out of sight now from suspected watching eyes, the Spanish Head turned north-west and with all hands on deck; as full sails bulged in the morning wind, and normality ensued as the crew returned to their usual duties. Everyone was relaxed, and with the gentle breeze turning into a fair wind, the ship turned north to head for the Celtic Sea, for home. Now a day out and reaching the choppy waters a hundred miles from the Irish coast, Poccabeady, who was coming to the end of the Afternoon Watch, let out a yell with the words that always causes shivers to run down the spine 'ship ahoy'. There, off the aft-port, could be seen the hazy outline of the large ship that had been tracking the Spanish Head and closing steadily. There were still a few hours till night and a possible escape, but if it were a race, the Spanish Head would soon be caught, so an escape was out of question. Capcifi gave the order to take in half the sails, and steady as you go, and light the fires of the oven; this would, hopefully, deter any investigation and discovery of the valuable hidden cargo, as the only entrance to the hidden brandy was the trapdoor under the now hot oven. It took the large ship another hour and a half to draw alongside, and then it became obvious that on board were a mixture of soldiers and custom's staff. In a booming voice, a menacing looking custom's man informed the crew of the Spanish Head that being outside of international waters they could not board but would 'escort' the Capcifi and the crew on their journey and come on board as soon as both the ships were inside territorial waters. As a gesture of good will and to install a certain harmony, Capcifi invited the officers and captain of the large ship to come on board for dinner and rum; the offer, after deliberation, was duly accepted. Croozefeast assembled the spit onto which was skewered one of the deer from the amply-stocked kitchen, and soon an inviting aroma permeated to the upper decks and beyond. Cattalin took charge of the helm as the captain and Intcaract, the Bosun, descended below decks to the captain's cabin. The rum was brought to the table by Beachcampken, who was under instructions to keep the liquid flowing, as a large platter containing a whole haunch of deer, was placed in front of the welcomed (unwelcome) guests. The evening went well, and as

Cattalin steered into the Celtic Sea, with dusk fast approaching, the Spanish Head turned north heading for the Irish Sea and into international waters. Instructions came from the large ship to drop anchor overnight and that a boarding party of customs personnel would come over at eight bells of the Morning Watch. On hearing this, Capcifi gave instructions to Croozefeast to light the oven fires two hours earlier and make sure that breakfast was being cooked when the customs men arrive so as to act as an obstacle to any investigations in that area. All to the hammocks, all hoping that the day goes well in the morrow. Cattalin had had more than a long day and little time for resting, but now, a well earnt sleep was welcome indeed. The morning came quickly and as everyone was up at first light, they were met with a small swell as the tides changed and the wind increased but nothing to worry about, only a little choppy.

The custom's men boarded the Spanish Head and there was no sign of the pleasantries shown the night before, and it looked like this was going to be an uneasy visit. Cattalin and some of the crew had settled around the oven and got stuck into a hearty breakfast, much to the envious eyes of the custom's officers as they passed to begin their search. The sharp questions, or actually orders, of the grumpy, stern officer called Arthenos were acted upon with expected haste by Intcaract as Beachcampken kept a close eye on the situation. The top deck had passed the inspection, the galley (where the oven is located) was apparently ignored with only a cursory glance being offered. Now, to the main storage hold were Intcaract hands over the legitimate bill of sale which accompanied the barrels of wine and, of course, the empty barrels to be used by the cider makers of the British mainland. Just a surly grunt from Arthenos greeted the paperwork as he ordered his men to count the barrels of wine, and with surprise, the count was thirty one, when the figure should have been an even thirty. Intcaract called for Cattalin to recount the barrels, and indeed, there are thirty-one heavy barrels and one less empty barrel than there should be; some head scratching followed. The custom's officer was not at all pleased as he yelled at his men to throw them all overboard. Emergency action was called for as Intcaract asked Cattalin to bring Capcifi to a rather difficult situation, and Capcifi, in turn, asked to speak to the captain of the large ship. The two captains met in the hold, and Capcifi was quite convincing in argument as he stated that there was an obvious mistake, and that if they were, indeed, smuggling barrels of wine, it would be more than one barrel, and that an occasional gift of an extra barrel was made by the sellers for the benefit of the Spanish Head's crew. With a suggestion that the offending barrel be removed and disposed of as the customs men thought would settle the situation, the captain of the large ship agreed and ordered Arthenos to throw the felonious barrel overboard. Arthenos, in turn, grunted some orders to the customs men and a barrel was duly removed, carried to the starboard bow and flung unceremoniously into the waves. One of them commented that the barrel had squealed as it descended to the sea; this raised a chuckle from both crews as the barrel bobbed up and down to and fro moving with the tide. That was it, all finished, and the custom's men left without noticing the hidden trap door under the now smouldering oven. The captain addressed the whole crew assembled on deck and thanked them all for their diligence and patience and explained about the barrel, which so nearly cost the loss of all the wine, and pointed towards the drifting tub bobbing a couple of hundred yards away. Then, at that very moment, there in the distance was a whistle, instantly recognised by Stoneyrama as a 'help me' signal; to which he sent out in reply a return high-pitched combination of whistles. Cattalin also heard the reply and realised that there was only one other person, that he knows, would and could communicate by that means; none other than his beloved Saramemara. There was sudden panic as Cattalin gesticulated towards the captain and shouted, in earnest, that the granddaughter of Ninida is out there and that, how and why, were of no consequence at the moment. The captain instructed the crew to turn the Spanish Head about and head for the barrel; this would take time as the wind was not blowing in a favourable direction. It was time for Ifauflogmen to come clean and explains to all present that he was sworn to secrecy by Saramemara, who wanted to surprise Cattalin at the end of the journey and hid, with the help of Ifauflogmen, inside one of the empty wine barrels drilled with small air holes. The young girl was kept nourished with food supplied by Ifauflogmen (hence the reason that he kept disappearing with half his food ration) all because Saramemara could not bear to be parted from her beloved Cattalin, any longer.

The Spanish Head slowly tacked to turn in the right direction, but it was quite obvious that the barrel was sinking, albeit gradually, lower and lower, and it looked as if the Spanish Head would not reach Saramemara in time. Feeling that he was responsible for the hapless girl, and that he was by far the strongest swimmer, and known that Cattalin could not swim at all, Ifauflogmen, without hesitation, leapt over the side. Another signal from Stoneyrama, by way of a combination of shrill whistles, filled in air and informed Saramemara that help was on its way. Half the crew were working feverishly moving the sails the other half line the port side yelling encouragement to Ifauflogmen, who was now within fifty yards of the barrel and closing fast. There was less than six inches of barrel showing as it was perilously close to disappearing into the grasp of Davy Jones' Locker and oblivion. The voices of encouragement had all but stopped as Ifauflogmen approached ten yards, eight yards, six yards as the barrel slipped gently beneath the waves. Almost there, Ifauflogmen dove, dolphin like, under the surface; thirty seconds later, up he came, took a deep breath and dove again and again as his feet were the last thing seen for Ifauflogmen, in vain, heroically tried to reach Saramemara. There was complete silence as the whole crew looked desperately for any sign, and not even Chairanseat, the carpenter, (who had taken position in the crow's nest) could see any sign of either the barrel or the gallant Ifauflogmen' they were lost, both had perished.

Three Times He Dived

Three times he dived,
So brave.
Three times he tried,
To save,
Third time he died,
In watery grave.

On reaching the Isle of Man, the melancholy crew went about their business, and although a good profit was made and shared, all would give it back in return of those lost. This was the last journey of Cattalin, the smuggler, who became a hermit and could be seen, on occasion, standing on the seashore, staring out to sea; listening for the whistling sound of his beloved Mariposa

160

(a sound that he swore could be heard when a strong wind blew inland across the waves).

Jonathan opens his eyes and once again, climbs out of his refuge—an old shopping trolley, looks about and seeing the area free of bullies, clambers out and walks homeward. Only those who have loved so deep could feel the emotion of loss; only those who have given their whole could feel the sense of sadness, remorse and disbelief that encompasses the mind, body and soul of the surviving partner. It is at times like this that words mean nothing, friendships are immaterial, that reality is none existent, and the loss is beyond comprehension; such is life, such is death. Jonathan, even though he has many experiences both good and bad, is speechless, speechless to the extent that he was struggling to even breathe. I advised that we take a break or even call it a day as I see his eyes were welling with tears, and he was suffering as if this tale was, at one time, indeed reality. The more I hear the recollections of my friend Jonathan, the more I am inclined to believe that these lives are true, and as he recalls more and more of them, I see the emotion that can only emanate from a person who has experienced, first hand, those situations, those feelings, those adventures encompassing love, sadness, joy and friendship.

Chapter 8
The Bed Is Vacant

Players: Butetil, Fichfanch, Namarind, Logeydeen, Patilin, Pigame, Hermono, Witte, Taligaw, Oniweg, Spollibon.

A bright day, and Jonathan is up with the larks, but before he can go out and enjoy himself, there are chores to be done but luckily, only one today, and that is to clean his bike until it sparkles and passes the inspection by his father. This done, off Jonathan went to meet up with friends and pick the early mushrooms in fields a couple of miles away. One of his friends lived just across the street, but Jonathan was forbidden, by his father, to associate with him; something to do with being from the wrong sort of family (it was noticeable that they were a little poorer). He was a great pal, and when it came to gathering chestnuts, the two of them used to be the ones that climbed to the highest branches and shake off the best 'conkers'; these we would sell to other children for a halfpenny apiece (pre-decimal coins of course); that was fun. Jonathan and his friend from across used to meet further away by a prior agreement made at school, on some occasions, the word would get back to his father that they were seen playing or riding their bikes together and receive smacked legs for disobeying. Jonathan lived in constant fear of punishments but decided that he could pick his own friends and was as careful as possible to keep out direct confrontation from father. Jonathan was even, for some unknown reason, not allowed to speak to the two girls from another family just across the street; they were fun to talk to and shared books and were pretty good at marbles as well. Jonathan remembers well the times the two girls and himself would cycle to the allotments and crawl under large patches of rhubarb hiding under the large leaves; they would cut the sweet tender stalks leaving the large leaves in place so no one could notice the rhubarb was missing. The stalks were then dipped into a bag of sugar and eaten there and then; that was fun and innocent to them at the time (luckily, nobody ever found out who the culprits were; that was our secret, good friends keep secrets, don't they?). Coming back from the mushroom hunting, there was not a sign of the expected interference from the local bullies; Jonathan and friends must have been too early for them that day. That was a good day, good fun, camaraderie at its best, and Jonathan thoroughly enjoyed the freedom. That evening as the family sat round the dining table, Jonathan recalls, in the room there was a television showing 'The Lone Ranger', black and white in those days, of course, and Jonathan leant a little to his left to see the screen when mother moved her seat slightly to allow full sight of the television. That was enough for his father to spring out of his seat and grab Jonathan viciously by the throat, yelling something like 'how dare you make your mother move' and dragged Jonathan outside and flung him up against the back wall of the house and told to stand there. A trickle of blood could be seen coming from a bad scratch on his neck, and the three children from next door, who were playing in their back garden, asked if he was alright. That was both humiliating and painful, but there was nothing that anyone could do, as that was the way of things; that was the norm. The following week was a quiet one for Jonathan as he kept away from his friends in fear of further punishment and had evaded the ever-present bullies by running whenever he caught sight of them. During the last couple of years, Jonathan had become one of the best cross-country runners in the region, which was a skill that none of the bullies could hope to match; in a fair race that is. All was good until one afternoon when Jonathan was singled out at the end of the school day, and being cornered, he was thrown into one of the thorn bushes at the edge of the playground. These were vicious thorns nearly two inches long, and they stuck sharp and deep, much to the delight of the bullies who left Jonathan to disentangle himself from the many barb-like darts of pain. Some of the thorns had broken leaving a dozen or so still embedded mainly in his back, legs and arms. Jonathan made his way home, every step aggravating his wounds and sores, and there, waiting at the end of his street, were the menacing bullies, but as Jonathan turned to escape, another bully blocked his escape. Quick thinking,

Jonathan hurdled a garden hedge and through the back garden of the nearest house, climbed a fence and ran; never minding the pain and flees to the woods to hide again. Curling up into the usual sanctuary, stinging with pain, Jonathan kept quiet and did not move an inch; he had outwitted them again but only just. Jonathan closed his eyes; there were no tears as Jonathan had virtually forgotten how to cry; he suggested that father would be proud of that.

Jonathan recalled that the next experience was an eye opener into the realm of care and caring, in so much that when he opened his eyes, he was now an elderly woman called Hermono, who was a well-read lady approaching eighty-five, sitting in a highchair within a large room and definitely not alone. Someone who appeared to be a nurse was shouting at a gentleman opposite 'Witte, eat your birthday cake'. Others in the room, well, half of them, were singing happy birthday and eighty-two today, eighty-two today. The establishment appeared to be either some sort old people's home or a hospital, and most of the patients had some sort of bandage around at least one of their limbs. Witte had a bandage on the left knee and a support stocking on the right knee, and he is sat in a wheelchair as he was approached by Namarind, who he believed was at least ten years his elder. Namarind propelling a Zimmer frame was sporting white support stockings, one on each leg, both of which had drifted towards the ankles, and a gown that was amply covered by her attempted efforts to consume chocolate-coated birthday cake. With the wheels locked on the wheelchair, there was no escaping from the pouted lips of Namarind as she planted a creamy smacker upon the right cheek of Witte with the accompanied comment of 'if I were fifty years younger, I'd give you a proper birthday treat'. Witte, with his usual witty, remarked a reply, 'if I were fifty years younger, you wouldn't be able to catch me'. Looking around the room, there are others as Jonathan described those present; Logeydeen, a person that could only be described as a 'man of the road' recovering from a broken leg; Fichfanch, a lady of means who had a broken hip who was constantly talking about how well her grandchildren were doing in their obviously important professions; Patilin, who was another in her late seventies, was chatty, but spent 90 percent of the time asleep and was well-known for suddenly waking up and carrying on with a subject of conversation which could be hours old. Just a little to the left side of Witte, sat Butetil who never said a word that was not a grumble; she moaned all day, every day, constantly, even if no one was actually listening. Some of the occupants were confined to bed, some from choice did not venture out of their rooms; although, they were encouraged by the nursing staff, to do so. There was one elderly lady who kept trying to escape, either out the doors or even climbing out of one of the windows; the staff had even tried keeping the bedsides up, but Oniweg soon clambered over that obstacle, not a recommended procedure to attempt with a recently broken hip. Everyone acted as lookouts and informed the nurses if they saw Oniweg 'on the run'; apparently, she thought that the 'mystery tour' bus would go without her. The youngest, by far, was Pigame who must be under thirty, the victim of a pretty bad fall from the horse she was riding and suffered a broken leg and some sort of back injury. A very fit young lady who was determined to the extreme and was almost permanently either trying to walk with the aid of crutches or laying on her bed doing various knee bending exercises. Jonathan recalls thinking that it must be great to be young; they heal quicker and have, on the whole, a more determined nature and most of all, the ability to handle the situation with a more positive attitude than the older generation. There was a new arrival due, or so according to the rumour circulating the rest-room, which would fill the last available bed. This awareness of something of interest or a change from the norm happening was the highlight of the day, in fact, of the week. Hermono had been an inpatient in this rehabilitation centre for over five weeks, and it was noticeable that conversation had all but dried up apart from the occasional mention of the weather. Most of the day was spent in silence broken by the regular ringing of buzzers and bells by those whose requirement was to visit the loos. This place was not the end of the road but merely one of the many crossroads in life, and of course, as one advances in years, the choices of which direction to take are rather more limited by the actual physical and mental state of the traveller. The realisation that, in this small but well-stocked rehabilitation centre, it had become apparent that some patients did not have a choice at all but were, steered, directed by the establishment to 'sunnier climes', some with a helping nudge from relatives who believed that they were 'doing the right thing' for whatever reason. Hermono had, since birth, lived in a large manor situated in a picturesque Warwickshire village; her father was the local doctor, and her family had lived in that property since 1650AD and the time of James II. She went to school in the village and was married in the spring of 1950, at the age of eighteen to a young teacher. Sadly, her husband died shortly after their celebrations for the fiftieth wedding anniversary; just one of the many long suffering victims of cancer. Since then, Hermono had lived alone; her pleasure was tending to the large garden and was particularly fond of the roses and proud to prune the apple trees; Hermono even had a ride-on mower for the large lawns, giving her much satisfaction in keeping up her husband's tradition of the 'best striped' lawn in the village. Now, here she was, separated from a lovely house, a beautiful garden, her paradise, her home, her world. Hermono did have a daughter who lived many miles away, a daughter who had visited once in five weeks and had for years, since the death of her father, tried to persuade her mother to sell up and downsize. That was one thing that Hermono blankly refused to do because after spending eighty plus years living in and lovingly tending for the house and grounds, wished to spend the rest of her life there. Hence, the rare visits by relatives who could not understand why Hermono endured the hardships of living and maintaining a very large property set in two acres of grounds. A few weeks previous, Hermono was enjoying a gin and tonic relaxing on one of the garden benches, not that she drank a lot, nothing more than two gins a day, when she saw something move by the far garden wall. On investigation, she came across a lone junkie shooting up; this young man had been chased away on numerous other occasions by Hermono. The young man had been chased from most gardens in the village; his name is Taligaw and was, by all words, harmless and polite but in a bad way after a few years of succumbing to drugs. He apologised as usual and slumped down just outside of the garden wall. Hermono returned to her garden seat and finished off her aperitif before venturing inside to prepare her evening meal, a small salad picked fresh from the walled vegetable garden.

The best stripes in the village.

There were noises coming from the drawing room, which should not be, because Hermono lived alone, and as she entered the room, there stood three persons, all dressed in black and wearing balaclavas; these were burglars, and two of them were holding baseball bats. Hermono screamed and left swiftly, a spritely specimen for her age, almost running out into the garden only to fall headlong down the two stone steps leading to the lawn; an audible crack could be heard as her left femur fractured, and her left clavicle broke in two as well as a twisted right ankle. The next thing Hermono knew was that she woke up in a hospital bed with arm in sling and leg in a temporary plaster cast. What a to-do; one of her neighbours had heard a commotion and made their way round only to see three figures disappearing down the lane but found Hermono and raised the alarm. That happened a few weeks ago, and now, here she was, in a rehabilitation centre recovering very slowly physically and even slower mentally; this was part due to the shock of the burglary and part despondency of losing her freedom and the security of familiar surroundings. All that happened now, on a daily basis, was the experience of being turfed out of bed only to be wheeled to the rest room (Hermono could not weight-bear on either leg yet so had to be manoeuvred by one of the nurses on a medieval-looking piece of equipment called a 'Sara Stedy') only to be sat in a high chair until it was time for bed. No garden, no gin, no roses to smell and no apples to pick; this was when the mind reverted to memories, not only memories of life and loves but memories of freedom, memories when she could walk in the village and smile. She had asked to be taken back home, but that appeared to be an impossibility as the OTs (Occupational Therapists) discounted such a move as Hermono would be 'home alone' and apparently, in an unsafe environment. This was a sad situation when freedom of choice was denied and the patient had no control of their life, with their wishes and needs completely ignored because it did not match the criteria of the authority. It was almost as if this was some sort of imprisonment but for 'the apparent good of the patient' which begs the question, whose choice was it anyway; now there's a thing; what a to-do? As Hermono sat, positioned between Oniweg and Patilin, there were only thoughts of the next ten hours matching the previous two or three weeks with Oniweg continuously wandering off to catch a tour bus and wanting to know why people were trying to stop her and Patilin opening her eyes every hour discussing the conversation of hours before. All Hermono could do was, because of being brought up in a society accustomed to a 'grin and bear it, attitude' to blend into a sort of twilight zone with the only expectation of escape being supper and bed. When Butetil entered the restroom, the whole congregation, as if it were a cognitive reaction, shut their eyes and pretended to be asleep; this seemed to be an encouragement for Oniweg to try another escape and chaotic scenes ensued. The dreariness was, for a few minutes, relieved as half-a-dozen staff searched frantically for the escapee who was eventually recovered from the front carpark, complete with Zimmer frame, still searching for the tour bus which would take her to the seaside. There were occasional respites when Pigame swiftly entered on her crutches made and drank a coffee, without sitting down and with a hearty cheerio disappeared just as quickly toward the various underused pieces of equipment in the gym. With regards to Butetil, who for the last hour had not stopped complaining about anything whether it be the draught from an open window or the lack of air, any political party, programmes on the television, the state of her hair, it would appear that the list was truly endless. Looking up, Hermono saw Fichfanch enter the restroom making a bee-line straight for the group of three; realising that they were a captive audience, Fichfanch approached with a new batch of photographs. These were flicked though as fast as possible and handed around the room, but Fichfanch pulled from her handbag an iPad which contained the most comprehensive collection of family and holiday photographs; now there was no flicking through as Fichfanch was the only one skilled enough to operate the ultimate weapon for use as a harbinger of boredom. Hermono, at this point, pretended to be asleep, but the agony continues as she could still 'hear' the countless boasting of the escapades and achievements of the families of others and wished a long-awaited wheel back for evening teatime. Obviously, Fichfanch was proud of her family but rather than inflicting others, should actually begin to wonder why members of her family had not visited in the four weeks of being an inpatient. It was not the first time that the thoughts of Hermono had a little sadness for the narrowness and falseness, almost self-denial of Fichfanch, who, quite obviously, must, deep down, be aware that her family were completely ignoring her demise. Hermono was concerned that she would never see her home or garden again but did retain that inner hope along with an expectation of returning to the familiar surroundings. Possibly, because that was all she had to hang on to, almost as a mentally-engineered reassurance that there must be a way to return, or was this it, an existence that was not an existence but more of a penance. There were long periods of nothingness as there was nothing more to say and even if there was, who was willing to listen or actually capable of listening. Jonathan relates that this life is not a life at all but a group of likeminded individuals surviving uneasily the twilights of once bright and fulfilling lives.

There was a moment of relaxation when Logeydeen was wheeled in, smelling a lot better than when he first arrived and had even been given a shave, removing a rather large beard; which was apparently moving on its own accord. He was quite a cheerful chap who was quick to explain that last night was the first time in a bed for four-and-a-half years and his first wash since slipping into a lake some ten months ago. Hermono thought to herself that he could tell a few tales of life, love and woe and looked forward to exchanging the trepidations of a person surviving life on the road. Which, of course, was far more interesting than thousands of personal photographs, but Logeydeen was rather a shy person; probably as a result his lifestyle, but one could only guess what hardships he had endured, how many cold winter nights he had spent shivering beneath the stars. Hermono got to thinking that here was Logeydeen who had experienced years of privations but was now, to him, living in luxury; so one person's perception of good living is another's nightmare. There were a few visitors arriving, mainly for the newcomers, and Hermono had noticed that most of the inpatients receive visitors in the first few days and then nobody for weeks on end, how sad. *'These were times,'* thought Hermono, *'when the old saying "a friend in need, is a friend indeed" came to mind, but in reality, any friend would be appreciated.'* Hermono thought back to when she first came into the rehabilitation complex and the many friends and neighbours who offered help; but for Hermono, it was all too evident that these were mere polite words, words of no substance and actions that were not forthcoming. The realisation of a situation which did not match the expectation is a shock to the system, and it is at times like this that your 'best friends' come into play; these are the vital components of survival, who will 'be there for you' not only in times of hardship and illness but always. The only downside is that as one advances in years, the already small list of these 'best friends' diminishes with time, and Hermono is down to two of these, friends that she can rely upon any time of day or night. Hermono turned towards Logeydeen and enquired if 'he' had any 'best friends' or indeed any friends at all, and the reply from this man of the road was a firm no but added that all the patients here appeared to be disenchanted with all their, so-called friends, where are they. With a twinkle in his eye Logeydeen swung his wheelchair around to leave, turned his head and looked Hermono straight in the eye and added some words of wisdom conveying that he was never disappointed by the lack of friends, visitors and relatives because if you hadn't got any, you cannot be disappointed by them for not visiting. Logeydeen got to the door and turned his head again and explained to one and all that his motto was 'everyday day is a good day if you're breathing' and departed to his room.

Another day in the ward, same as every day before: bed wash, breakfast, chair and that was the morning done, but there were more rumours that someone else was coming, and all those present in the restroom were wondering who was leaving, who's bed was being vacant. Looking around, there was an obvious gap were Oniweg always sat, so enquiries were made to one of the helpers, and it came to light that Oniweg was last night transferred to a 'care home'. Those two words that, to the majority of inpatients, were met with trepidation as it often meant the coup-de-grâce move on a person's chessboard of life; to Hermono, it was the none availability of choice, coupled with the actual finality of it all; that was hard to accept. The arrival of the new patient ambulance caused a stir, but no-one could see enough to catch a glimpse of the new patient as the trolley was wheeled by into Oniweg's old room. It was not until lunch, when more patients assembled in the restroom including Logeydeen, who informed them all that there had been a shuffle around because the new patient was a male, and Oniweg was in one of the double occupancy rooms with another women, and the two men had now been moved to the double-bedded room. Of course, Logeydeen was grilled by the other patients for all the gist on the new occupant, and all he could tell at that moment was that the man was probably in his early twenties and had been the victim of a rather vicious attack, resulting in a fractured lower arm, a nasty broken leg and a couple of broken ribs for good measure. A brave young man who reminded Logeydeen of himself many years ago when he was footloose and fancy-free; until he met a like-minded young lady whom he eventually married. Logeydeen opened up a little, almost apologetically, and explained that his wife had died from cancer over ten years ago and, out of remorse, had since then been 'travelling' aimlessly throughout the land. Later that morning, the young man made an appearance, wheeled in on a transfer chair by one of the nurses, like a lamb to slaughter and the first to attach, limpet like, was Butetil closely followed by Fichfanch, almost forming a queue. Coming to the rescue, Logeydeen gently but forcefully steered his self-propelled wheelchair between the young man and at least two totally unwanted, unneeded, uncalled-for verbal assaults and asked the carer to wheel the young man to a safer place in the restroom. This was witnessed by Hermono who believed she recognised the young man and turned towards the far corner of the restroom for a second look and confirmed her first thoughts. At the same time, the young man glanced towards the group of three ladies and shouted over to Hermono a hearty greeting of 'hello lady', to which Hermono gave reply 'see what happens when you take drugs' after the realisation that the young man now in a wheelchair was none other than Taligaw whom she had chased from her large garden more than once and turned her head away, pretending to converse with the now sleeping Patilin. It was almost an hour later when Taligaw was wheeled back to his shared room, and on passing, Hermono wished her a good evening.

Everyone was returning to their own rooms in readiness for the evening snack, which was a choice of various fillings for freshly-made sandwiches with a small yogurt for afters; nothing fancy but enough to last until breakfast. Hermono was just getting ready to leave the restroom when Logeydeen drew up alongside her and expressed that, in his opinion, she was a little harsh towards Taligaw, especially in the circumstances.

Wondering what was meant by that remark, Hermono responded that she had known Taligaw for many years and considered him to be a burden to society and no more than a nuisance in her village. To this, Logeydeen asked if she had ever tried to hold a conversation with this 'nuisance of the village', and Hermono retorted with a stern 'certainly not' and looked Logeydeen in the eye and asked him outright as to what right he had to question her or her actions and bid Logeydeen good night. Only the right of the freedom of speech, dear lady, was Logeydeen's reply and added with the belief that we are all equals on this earth in the context that we, who are born, will die; the bit in between are the cards we are dealt, and that 'the many' have little choice of how to play the hand, and that guidance is the key, and it is this guidance or lack of it that sometimes excludes poor souls such as I and the brave Taligaw. It gave Hermono a little thought for the night as she did not really mean to cause offence, but her situation had begun to make her more than a little stern, and unlike her, her situation had begun to alter her opinions. Hermono rested her head on the soft pillow and recapped the evening's conversation and hoped, deep inside, that she was not becoming a stereotype 'old person' who attacked the world because they were losing, albeit slowly, their own rights; rights to choose, rights to where she could live, rights to handle their own affairs and retaliate by hitting out at authority and anyone else who treaded upon their path. After breakfast and the all too regular, wheeling to the restroom, Hermono was again settled in for the day but with a determination to not become the bitter being who went to bed the night before, after the realisation that it could be a slippery slope; an all too easy path to descend. With a little resolve, Hermono was the first to offer a cheery good morning as Logeydeen approached; this was greeted with the pleasantness it deserved, resulting in Logeydeen joining her for a morning cuppa. Hermono even offered an apology for her sudden tirade directed at fellow patient Taligaw, to which Logeydeen nodded his head as an accepted approval and offered the wise words 'sometimes the mouth speaks rubbish when you feel rubbish'; to counteract that feeling Logeydeen said that he thought of one of the best sensations he knows all too well, as a man of the road, was that of 'petrichor''. This was a statement that Hermono understood, but that in itself did not give her the incentive to condone the use of drugs or actually the misuse of drugs. To this, Logeydeen agreed but accepted that not all people are strong enough to evade such things, and at times, the use is nothing more than an escape from whatever ails either the mind, the body or even both. Just as the two finished this short conversation, a police officer entered looking for Taligaw and was pointed in the right direction; this produced a comment from Hermono which was again a little sharp. There was no conceivable need for such a comment, but again, Hermono spoke not from the heart but from a store of self-opinionated preconceptions, indicating that Taligaw was receiving his comeuppances because of his use of drugs. This comment prompted a reply from Logeydeen, in defence of Taligaw; he informed Hermono that the visit from an officer of the law had little to do with the use or misuse of drugs, and that it was the actions of Taligaw that were of interest. This caused a look of bewilderment from Hermono, and a certain amount of intrigue had developed, so it was of little wonder that Hermono had asked Logeydeen to enlighten her as to the meaning of such a statement. Being roommates, Taligaw and Logeydeen had got on really well, with Logeydeen discussing the ups and downs of living by wits and fortitude. Taligaw quietly imparting the misfortunes of a drug addict; the result of a sad upbringing and an inevitable journey down the wrong track. The only difference between the two, less fortunate souls, was that the lifeway that Logeydeen had chosen was voluntary, and the pathway of Taligaw appeared to have been somewhat hereditary (Taligaw had been fed drugs from an early age by his parents, and that was the path given). Sitting back, with a cup of tea in hand, Logeydeen sipped gently before looking Hermono in the eye and told her exactly what happened to the unfortunate Taligaw. On an evening a few weeks ago, Taligaw had told his roommate that after being chased from the garden of a large house by the genteel lady, he had sat down and whittled a piece of wood to form a shape of a squirrel (one of the passions, in fact, his greatest love, was working with wood); he noticed some people dressed in black loitering near the garden gate; three of them pulled on balaclavas and walked toward the house. It was then that Taligaw heard the shouts of the old lady, who had half an hour before chased him from the garden; without any hesitation, Taligaw ran to the rescue, but 'three against one' made short odds. It was this gallant attempt to offer assistance to the lady of the house that led to a terrible beating by three baseball bats leaving a battered body bravely broken below the wall. This young man could have just walked away; he had troubles enough of his own, but there are times when you cannot turn your back and run away from life, as he had been doing since an early age. There was a look of realisation in the face of Hermono as 'the penny dropped' that Taligaw had actually attempted to help her and obviously with little regard for his own safety. *'Am I mean and thoughtless?'* thought Hermono, *'no to the first but maybe, no, not maybe, but yes to the latter?'* It is a little difficult for someone who has always had everything to imagine having, materialistically, nothing at all; let alone an unstable mental outlook. Hermono told Logeydeen that she would personally speak to Taligaw tomorrow and will give the matter great thought before they meet and even asked Logeydeen to both arrange a meeting and accompany Taligaw. The next morning arrived slowly for Hermono, whose mind had been more-than-a-little overactive during the night; the result being that Hermono slept little accompanied with a realisation that growing old was more complicated than anticipated. This was something that required a multiplicity of skills, skills that were not taught but eventually obtained through trial and error, and in the case of Hermono, more error than trial. If only there was a book in which the procedure of obtaining an active coping mechanism was explained.

One by one, the patients appear in the restroom, pushing Zimmers, self-propelled wheelchairs, and others being wheeled in; a fine example of suffering humanity. Hermono looked around and realised that some of the patients were aware of what was happening, some just didn't know what was happening, others didn't care, and some just couldn't do anything to change the outcome. Hermono reflected on her own dilemma which was a combination of all the aforementioned. Hermono thought long and hard at this supposition presented by herself, and the reality was (1) she was aware of what was happening; her daughter wanted the house whether it be to live in or to sell, (2) she did not know if she would be forced into a care home, (3) she cared deeply for the freedom she once had, (4) she was deeply worried that she would have no say in the outcome. All of these things swimming around in her head had begun to turn Hermono into a bitter and twisted old lady; something that she never was, and something that she regretted, but now there were sparks of willpower, determination and solace firing in the furnaces of the brain. As Taligaw approached, there was a worried look on his face, a look of trepidation, this was because he had had a lifetime of confrontation, rejection and distrust, and it was 'not' something that he was at all accustomed to or enjoyed but usually suffered (as a result of hatred and bigotry) in quiet acceptance. It appeared that Logeydeen had not enlightened young Taligaw as to the subject of this meeting with Hermono, and before Hermono could speak, Logeydeen joined the two, complete with three teas on a tray accompanied by a selection of biscuits. A man of the road he may be, but a heart of gold and a mind as sharp as a tack; Logeydeen had thought it not his place to pass on second-hand information. Hermono shakenly held her cup with both hands, took in a swallow of well-sugared tea and held out her hand towards the young Taligaw; this was an act of peace-making. There was no movement from Taligaw, probably, because he had never encountered such a thing, but he was an expert in rejection, refusal and just did not know how to react to an act of kindness. It was time for Logeydeen to intervene, who had a word in the ear of a nervous Taligaw and explained that Hermono was trying in her own way to say sorry, sorry for misjudging, sorry for projecting a stereotypical assumption and sorry for causing extra grief to an already delicate situation. The result was an outstretched hand from young Taligaw, and with a reciprocal action from Hermono, all looked well. Hermono explained that she had no idea whatsoever of the act of bravery and thanked Taligaw profusely. This gave Taligaw an opportunity to give a nervously-presented family history; I suppose as some sort of justification for his lifestyle. A second cup of tea was served by Logeydeen, who, by this time, sported a bit of a grin in appreciation to how well his two patient friends were now getting on. During her near sleepless night, Hermono had thought through a number of scenarios and had come to the conclusion that a reward should be forthcoming; but to be diplomatic, she asked Taligaw if he would accept a reward in appreciation for his bravery. It was made clear by Taligaw that his actions were made not for monitory gain but with a sense of commitment for the protection of a fellow human being, especially a vulnerable soul such as an elderly lady. Just as Hermono leant forward to reply, in walked her daughter Spollibon, on only her second visit to the rehabilitation centre; Hermono looks towards her fellow patients to let them know that this conversation is far from over.

Hermono greeted her daughter and thanked her for the visit, but Spollibon seemed a little anxious as she sat down next to her mother and began to explain that a care home had been arranged, and that it would be a good idea if the big house was put up for sale. This had come as a shock to Hermono but deep down an expected outcome and one, because of her present situation, that she felt compelled to comply. A moment of thought from Hermono resulted in a reply that could only be described as a desperate postponement of acceptance and indicated that she would 'sleep on it', and that there was no rush. Spollibon left soon after hearing that negative response. Now, Hermono realised why the Matron had mentioned, only a couple of days before, that even with progress there was no one at home, and at the recent 'Care Team' meeting, it had been recommended that transfer to a 'Care Home', whenever and wherever a vacancy occurred, was the next move. The conversation was heard by the fellow patient, Fichfanch, who sat down beside Hermono and apologised that she could not help overhearing, and that she too was in the same boat as all her children wanted her manor house or actually the money. Fichfanch enquired if Spollibon had 'Power of Attorney' over her mother, to which Hermono quietly replied that she had refused point blank to pass any power to her daughter, just in case control over the more important decisions, concerning her home, her finances or anything else for that matter, were not to her liking. It soon came to light why Fichfanch had asked, as she had given her eldest 'Power of Attorney' months ago, and unfortunately, her eldest (with assistance from her other children) were trying their very best to have her sent to a care home, permanently, and there was little she can do about it. With some trepidation Fichfanch was to be transferred to a Care Home some thirty miles from where she now lived, all arranged by her children because this would be, supposedly, 'for her benefit' regarding health and safety

177

concerns, and that she would be leaving the rehab centre in two days' time. Looking around, Hermono took note of the clientele, 80% were what you would call old and most of these were vulnerable and prime suspects for long-term care, which seemed to be the expected demise of vast numbers of the elderly populous. That night, Hermono had again little sleep and could not, in her mind, bring herself to leave her treasured home and would fight tooth and nail to keep it and live there to the end. There bred a glimmer of hope, in the form of an idea, a little spark of belief, a cunning plan, an escape route and an adventure to boot. As Hermono rested a weary head on a soft duck-down pillow, she finally felt a worthwhile life was still available; a goal was set, and by Jove she was determined to succeed. Another day dawned as Hermono was 'up with the lark' and already in the dayroom sipping at a cup of instant coffee made by one of the staff; in front of her laid out with purpose was a large writing pad and two pens, and she was awaiting for Taligaw and Logeydeen to show their faces. The two arrived, one pushed by a nurse and the other walking with a frame, and the first thing that was said by young Taligaw was that he accepted the apology offered by Hermono the day before; Hermono nodded her head in approval. There was a glimpse of a smile across the weather-beaten face of Logeydeen as he felt life was better with a cheery smile rather than a defensive frown and asked if anyone else in the dayroom wanted a cup of tea; with no takers Logeydeen settles in his chair. Hermono, nonchalantly, enquired as to what the pair of gentlemen sitting before her anticipated for the future. To which, Logeydeen implied, by his answer, that he was getting too long in the tooth for many more years on the road and felt that he may end up in some sort of care home just like Fichfanch, who was whisked away during the early hours; as her bed was, this morning, vacant. Enquiries were made to the staff who confirmed that Fichfanch would not be coming back. That's what happened at rehabilitation centres; get them in, and get them out, in readiness for the next one. Taligaw had been listening to the hardships that Logeydeen had witnessed and realised that this was no future to be looking forward to and would prefer a more stable and healthy lifestyle.

There was an offer on the table from Hermono in so much that she had six bedrooms, three of which had en suite, and, as

Taligaw was aware that there were large gardens, so one of the main reasons the daughter was reluctant for her mother to remain in the large house was that she was more than a little vulnerable. So, how would Taligaw and Logeydeen like a roof over their heads and an opportunity to begin a new life. There would, of course, be guidelines: Taligaw would have to attend counselling sessions primarily to take him off drug dependence, and both Taligaw and Logeydeen would be allocated a social worker to help with the transition from the 'path of self-destruction' to an environment of a stable, healthy and mentally-pleasing life. The offer included the full use of the house and garden, a job for Taligaw as a trainee carpenter with a local firm (on condition, he kicked his unfortunate habit), and Logeydeen, because of his love of the outdoors, would take the title of resident head gardener. These were the offers presented by Hermono who asked nothing more than an honest reply as all three would gain something, not least that Hermono would, hopefully, be able to live out her days in her home; that was all she wants, all she needs, all she could hope for. No immediate answer was required as Hermono asks the two lost souls to talk about it, sleep on it and let her know in due course. At that very moment, Patilin opened her eyes and spoke out, "Two sugars, please and one biscuit." This did cause a chuckle, not that anyone was laughing directly at Patilin but at the 'moment', and Witte rescued the situation by offering to make a cup for Patilin, but by the time Witte had accomplished the task, Patilin was, again, asleep. A day passed, and Hermono had heard nothing from either Taligaw or Logeydeen, and it was not until lunchtime on the second day that she was joined by two serious-looking patients. It was Logeydeen who took the roll of spokesperson and carried in his left hand an A4 sheet of paper which appeared to be half full of writing and written down were a number of questions. The first question was: 'what would happen if either of them slipped back into their old ways?' Second question: 'how much do they get paid?', and the last question: 'why us?' So to answer these questions in order, Hermono took a couple of minutes and addressed the two prospective housemates; firstly, there were no second chances just adhere to the requests, and all will be fine and dandy; the ball was in their court. To the second question, Hermono stated that there would be no wages for Taligaw, from her, only what he earned from the carpentry business, and that Logeydeen would receive proper wages for a head gardener, and both Logeydeen and Taligaw would be provided with accommodation at no cost, facilities at no cost, and that both or either of them could leave anytime they wished. The final question was answered thus. Hermono saw before her two people who had suffered for many years, and now there was literally a 'once in a lifetime' opportunity, actually an opportunity for all three. Hermono felt as if she owed something to humanity because of her lifetime of privileged living, and this was her chance to actively repay that privilege. The few weeks that Hermono had spent, as an inpatient, in the rehabilitation centre had given her time for thought, thoughts of others and a realisation that all that matters were not her alone.

Taligaw and Logeydeen looked at one another, and it was obvious that they had discussed at length the offers 'on the table', and both had wholeheartedly agreed to accept, and that this was an opportunity that could not be missed; a thank you from all three, to all three ensued.

Within a couple of weeks, there were more beds vacant as Hermono, Taligaw and Logeydeen began a 'new' life in the large house, and the last memory that Jonathan recalls is a scene rich in symbolism and meaning, On the garden bench could be seen Hermono with her glass of gin, her leg outstretched (a leg that had recovered badly), and on seats either side, sat, on the left, Taligaw with a pint of real ale and on the right, Logeydeen with a large cup of fennel tea. An unlikely trio thrown together in the wheel of life, each now dependent on the other, but all are free to follow whichever path they wanted or needed. Taligaw had found a meaning to his being, now with a job, and not only that, a job he enjoyed and felt fulfilling. Logeydeen had attained a sense of worth as he had now committed himself to working within and for the community; any job, any task, and the only reward was his self-esteem and a sagacity of purposeful existence. This was the moment that Jonathan opened his eyes and sat up in the shopping trolley, he wondered how it all worked out, and if he would ever go back some day. Even though Jonathan, in this life 'Hermono', was elderly, infirm and in fear of losing a home that contained both memories and a sense of belonging, he confided in me that this was a good meaningful life he would have no hesitation in returning to, if it was at all possible. It is now apparent to Jonathan that what matters is not power, wealth, pride, greed, hatred or ignorance but love, compassion and learning is all that is needed.

The Epilogue
The Journey Begins

There are, during a lifetime, many journeys that must be both contemplated and performed, whether planned or unexpected. It is how the traveller accepts that the option taken is the correct choice, which is not always obvious at the outset. Even on a straight road, when the objective appears to be a forgone conclusion, a deviation is unavoidable, and it is the preparation, alertness and the ability to change direction that is the key. Accept the situation, receive with open mind that any alterations to what you originally thought was 'your path' is for a purpose; sometimes not at all immediately fully comprehensible, but the reason is there, and may at times seem rather frivolous. Jonathan has learnt many things on these travels, such as: comradery, love, friendship, pain, despair, joy, sadness, trust, mistrust, skills and hopefully, a little wisdom. All this is a sort of life package, a package that the vast majority would experience, but a fraction of the knowledge that Jonathan has gathered over many a lifeway.

At the age of eighteen, Jonathan was old enough to vacate the family home and fend for himself, leaving the place where he was brought up, literally, by the scruff of his young neck. By a young age, Jonathan had lived many lives, that were now but memories, but isn't that what life actually is, a linearity of memories? The shortest thing in life is 'the now', and 'now' that is something that never actually happens but is, in reality, either the past or the future 'the now' does not exist. So, there is an enigma within an enigma because if 'now' does not exist, does anything exist, and if it does, is it but a memory, are we all living a memory; a memory in search of a future or, indeed, a future in search of a past? Jonathan had done well with studies and looked forward to university as he headed out of the small town, where he was born, taking not one glance behind, only looking forward. Unlike many of his friends, who headed to the large cities in search of the, all too often, mythical fame and riches, Jonathan made his way towards a few more years of study. This was an opportunity for Jonathan, not only to escape from a family background of argument and bickering but also a release from the constant worries of victimisation suffered at the hands of members of humanity who think that pleasure and enjoyment involves witnessing and causing the demise of fellow beings. The very thought of putting behind him, an episode in his life, a chapter filled at times with fear and trepidation, was enough to feel elated. This was not, really a form of escapism but, somewhat, a kind of enlightenment; almost as if it were a separation from one lifeway to another as if it were, indeed, another 'tale' and another 'shopping trolley' moment!

This was all now behind him, although, the memories will live long, and the actions of others will sit deep in the soul; such is life. It is now that Jonathan will rely upon the information gained and emotional experiences encountered during all of his past lives. The subjects that Jonathan will study at university, matching in part some of the stories, are History and Environmental Sciences. Matching an interest in cultural awareness with association to ancient and historical crafts and occupations. As a hobby, Jonathan has an interest in athletics and long distance walking, not that he is still 'running away from bullies' but because Jonathan has developed a sort of 'oneness' with the land, especially woodland; I wonder why? Jonathan has made it quite clear to me that these tales are not the total of the lives he has lived, and that maybe one day he will tell of a few more, but there is no pressure from me; the choice is his and his alone. There were times when I read through my notes of these tales and realised that the more I read, the more I believe that they are true. It is not in my remit to judge the authenticity of any of these tales; my purpose is to act as a mediator and scribe and leave the rest up to the readers of the **'Tales of Jonathan'**.

"There are times when life is but a memory and there are times when life is 'the now'; 'the now' being an amalgam of all that has gone 'before' and therefor the 'before' is an integral part of the future." PGS.

Live life true, with 'Love', 'Compassion' and 'Learning' as your goals; you never know when you are due to wake up and find yourself in some remote forest attempting to clamber out of a 'shopping trolley'.

****

Key to the Character Names

So that the anonymity of the characters (as listed at the beginning of each chapter) remains protected, they have been given anagrams of the subject matter from the lists below.

As an added challenge, the reader could attempt to solve the anagrams, of which, there are ninety-three; there is no prize for the correct answers, just the satisfaction of completing the task.

Chapter 1, Wildlife:
Players: Gheghedo, Suemo, Love, Quirsler, Reah, Bartib, Tapeloc, Darbeg, Greatbelonda, Grasylee, Tar.

Chapter 2, Trees:
Players: Percus, Dowerdo, Penijur, Prycess, Hebec, Erios, Olinagma, Thunkbroc, Lemtry, Raplop, Thutscen, Vengamor, Lawtun.

Chapter 3, Fish:
Players: Poglerbea, Katse, Pidlarch, Rotut, Raggynil, Kepi, Ebblar, Goguden, Lumtel, Harco, Monlas.

Chapter 4, Rocks:
Players: Chantitera, Chilti, Tandoness, Tablas, Tomiledo, Fraspled, Nariteg, Singeo, Phetomamric, Tiquatrez, Lottesuria.

Chapter 5, Waterways:
Players: Beckaria, Shanakew, Nella, Holmenca, Lishlag, Anvo, Neeba, Yeniblod, Deladuc, Dosiwec.

Chapter 6, Insects:
Players: Grantiplis, Fymyla, Syfelldam, Goldyfran, Shappergors, Cetrick, Egwari, Bludigesh, Daphi, Trelbytuf, Bebelumbe, Cripnoos.

Chapter 7, Salt water:
Players: Poccabeady, Beachcampken, Ifauflogmen, Capcifi, Cattalin, Intcaract, Ninida, Otiunderstars, Stoneyrama, Saramemara, Chairanseat, Croozefeast, Arthenos.

Chapter 8, Birds:
Players: Butetil, Fichfanch, Namarind, Logeydeen, Patilin, Pigame, Hermono, Witte, Taligaw, Oniweg, Spollibon.

I will talk to Jonathan again, soon.
Bye for now.
PGS